HAUNTED

by

Maria Savva

Printed and bound by Lulu.com 2012

Published by: Rose & Freedom Books
P.O. Box 55285
London N22 9EU
England, U.K.

Copyright © Maria Savva 2012

Cover design: © Maria Savva 2012

A catalogue record of this book is available from the British Library

ISBN: 978-0-9564101-7-7

Acknowledgements

Susan Helene Gottfried, thanks for all your hard work with the editing. Your comments and suggestions helped me to fine tune the novel. Thanks for pointing out the fact that Nigel's mind had a mind of its own!

Darcia Helle, thank you for being an eagle-eyed beta reader. You spotted lots of those dreaded typos. Thanks, particularly for mentioning the continuity issue with the plastic bin bag. That even slipped past the editor! Those gremlins are very cunning. Thanks also for saying Haunted is "brilliant" coming from such a talented writer as yourself, that is a massive compliment! I hope that many readers will agree with you :)

Susan Buchanan, thanks for being a great beta reader. You were so thorough and the things you pointed out about contraction of words in the dialogue will serve me well in future projects. I do have a habit of making people sound too formal! Must be the lawyer in me! Also, thanks for pointing out that Paulo should be Pablo - your multi-lingual abilities are priceless. Also thanks for spotting the clanger, where I used infamous to mean *really* famous!! Oh, dear!

Julie Elizabeth Aldridge, thank you so much for reading the book and for your comments. Thanks also for your continued support. It means a lot to me that one of my favourite authors also enjoys my books!

Calum McDonald, thank you for offering to beta read, and I'm impressed that you read the book in one sitting! I hope you're right that this is a 'hot' one :) I'm so glad you enjoyed it.

Michael Radcliffe, thanks so much for reading the book and your very helpful suggestions. Thanks also for being such a supportive friend. I am so pleased you enjoyed Haunted.

Joel Blaine Kirkpatrick, thank you so much for taking time out of your busy reading schedule to beta read Haunted. I appreciate that so much. Thanks for spotting that Nigel had a brother that I never knew he had LOL. He sneaked into the book when I wasn't looking. I got rid of him. Thanks also for pointing out the other errors. You have a very good editor's eye.

Wiz Green, thank you for reading through the pre-publication copy and your helpful comment about the computer game that Nigel was playing before it had been invented. As this wasn't meant to be a time-travel novel, I got rid of that LOL. I'm so glad you enjoyed the novel; thanks also for helping with the promotion!

Every day, crimes are committed in the heat of the moment. In that moment, the mind blurs, emotions are exaggerated, and control is out of reach. In that moment, when the crime is committed, the criminal sees a justification for the action. He or she is angry. There has been a word said or something done that creates a reason, propels them to carry out the crime. These are the flash crimes, those that are not premeditated. The ones that are planned are another story. The mind that plans the crime may be more able to deal with the consequences, or maybe the mind that plans the crime is already lost, so the crime cannot cause any further damage. For those who commit the unplanned murders, they are the ones who become tainted, scarred, lost. They will forever look back to that one moment in time and are doomed to live a life looking backwards, wondering why, wishing they could change the past. But time does not forgive these crimes, and the mind will pay the price.

Chapter 1

Nigel returned home from work at 9 p.m. As he closed the front door behind him, he could hear the familiar music that always made his stomach turn. His wife June enjoyed watching the programme. It was her favourite: *Crimewatch.* Each week, her eyes were glued to the TV screen, unmoving, transfixed, watching reconstructions of crimes that had taken place. Nigel hated it.

'I have to deal with enough stress in my life, why would I want to come home and watch such a depressing programme? Can't we watch something else?' His pleas were made in a moderate tone; Nigel had learnt the hard way that it did not pay to get angry. Anger was the seed that grew into hate, and hate was evil. The last twenty years of his life, he had been living as a shadow of his former self; afraid to live, guilt catching him at every turn. A cycle of fear, regret, and shame. A deep feeling that he did not deserve to even be living.

Nigel sometimes felt like a victim, but he would find himself unable to allow such thoughts further than the outermost regions of his mind. If they got any deeper, they would be met by the constant companion he now lived with; the one that reminded him, every time he breathed, that he was unworthy.

Twenty years ago, Nigel had been a young man, with prospects. In his early thirties he worked for a large company as an I.T. specialist. He would deal with all the computer problems and was paid a hefty amount to do so. He'd always been gregarious. He'd been confident and quick to speak his mind, quick to argue his case; he'd never been one to back down in an argument.

Now, Nigel was in his fifties. If you saw him walking along the street, you might be forgiven for thinking he was homeless. He didn't really care much about his appearance. He'd worked from home after his nervous breakdown for a couple of years, but his wife said that she thought he would benefit from going out to work because his bouts of depression were becoming more frequent. He was offered a job in London, over an hour on the train from where they lived. The train was the only transport he would use now. Not a car. Never a car. Not even a bus. The memories gave him no peace.

Nigel was living, but not really living. It was as if his soul had deserted him twenty years ago; a light had gone out inside him. He could never be the same.

He never raised his voice nowadays. In fact, his tone had become so quiet it was sometimes hard to tell if he was speaking. His lips would move, but it was as if the volume had been turned down. Maybe it was the screams he often heard in the night? The ones that would shake him from his dreams. The dreams that were, in reality, nightmares.

Nigel could not remember the last time he'd really slept; not without sleeping pills, anyway. It was as if his life had stopped twenty years ago. Someone else had died, but she had taken a piece of him with her.

Maybe that was what happened. If you killed someone, did they get to take your soul with them? Nigel often thought that was what must have happened. He'd had a lot of time to think about it. It was all he ever thought about.

Her face, her eyes. The look of shock in her eyes. That was the thing that lived in his conscience. Why? He had asked himself the same question many times, until it had driven him into a corner. He had not been able to live with himself. His mind had closed down.

June looked up at Nigel, who was standing at the hallway entrance to the lounge. 'You never used to be such an old bore, Nige,' she said, turning back to watch the programme. Then she twisted around again, quickly, as if she had just remembered something. 'There was a time we used to watch *Crimewatch* together, and any other programme that had anything to do with law and order. Remember we used to have fun?' She shook her head. 'Fun. Huh. Remember what that is? But, yes, we used to have fun laughing at all the rogues that got caught. Why are you so distant these days, Nige? We hardly spend a moment together anymore.'

Although the room was dark, only illuminated by a table lamp and the TV screen, he was sure he could see tears glistening at the edges of her eyes.

'It's always the same. You walk in from work and disappear into the kitchen, or the other room. Why, Nige?'

He hadn't expected this. He couldn't remember the last time he and June had exchanged two words with each other. An actual conversation was pushing it. He tried to answer, but any response he gave would be futile. He could not venture into a conversation with her now or ever. That part of his life was over for good. He shrugged, and mumbled, 'I'm going to make some pasta,' then disappeared into the kitchen.

Nigel sat at the kitchen table half an hour later. June's earlier rant filled his mind, momentarily taking precedence over the incessant chanting that reminded him of his guilt.

She was right. Years ago, they would laugh together. Quite a lot. They had been a fun couple to be around, he knew that because they were forever being invited to friends' houses, out to dinner, to parties and celebrations. They hardly spent any time in the house. Weekends were always taken up with hosting dinner parties or visiting friends, city breaks to destinations all over Europe—occasionally alone and enjoying each other's company, but more often with other couples. They'd had a hectic and satisfying social life. That all came to an end quite abruptly after he killed Emily Baxter.

He spooned some penne into his mouth and ate reluctantly. Eating was just another thing he had to do; he derived no satisfaction anymore, as if to enjoy anything now would be a sin. He was reminded of the way he used to be, and he wished he had listened to friends and family when they had warned him that his headstrong attitude would get him into trouble one day... if he'd had a penny for every time someone had said that... but he hadn't listened.

As he chewed his pasta, Nigel remembered the first time he had been warned about his behaviour. He had been ten years old, at a friend's birthday party. Jonah was celebrating his tenth birthday. He had received a remote-controlled car as a gift from his parents. Nigel asked him if he could play with it. 'No, it's my present,' said Jonah, sticking out his tongue.

Nigel watched as the boy pressed the button and the car zoomed around a track. He could feel an emotion that was not yet fully formed but was to become very familiar as he grew up: it was the first time he could remember feeling angry. His own parents did not allow him to have many toys. They said that it cluttered up the house, and besides he "didn't need so many toys". That wasn't the way Nigel saw it. He resented his parents' attitude. They were quite well off, from what he could gather. The family took holidays twice a year to visit his mother's family in Cyprus and his father's family who had emigrated to Spain from England. Many times, he remembered as a boy, his mother telling his aunts not to buy him any more toys. They never had birthday parties for him. 'It will only mean all his friends' parents will bring lots of tacky toys and we'll end up having to give them to a charity shop,' he heard his father say one day.

Nigel thought his parents were boring. Whenever he visited his cousins' houses, they had playrooms filled to the brim with toys, and their parents were always buying them more, even though he knew that his aunts and uncles were not very wealthy. He envied his cousins. His parents hardly ever took him to visit them anyway; they were always complaining about something one of his aunts had said and finding a reason not to visit. The truth was, his father didn't like his mother's sisters and would refuse to visit them; he thought they would be a bad influence on Nigel. In Nigel's mind, however, he was convinced the real reason his parents didn't want him to visit his cousins was because they didn't want him to ask for toys. He would always ask for toys after visiting them, feeling the void in his own life. He often heard his parents say that his aunts and uncles were spoiling their children; Nigel didn't understand what that meant, but in his heart, he felt neglected and deprived.

As he had watched Jonah's new red car speed around the track, his blood boiled in a way he had never experienced before. Suddenly, he lurched forward and grabbed the car from the track, throwing it sideways without looking. It ended up smashing against a glass cabinet that shattered. Some crystal glasses that were displayed in the cabinet had been knocked over, too.

'Nigel!' he heard his mother scream. She ran towards him and grabbed his arm, shaking him. 'Why did you do that?'

She turned towards the other parents and children who were all now silently watching the spectacle. The mother of a four year old who had been standing next to the glass cabinet, was wiping fragments of glass off the child's sweater, her face bright red and full of concern.

'I'm so sorry,' said Nigel's mother to the crowd of onlookers. 'We're going home now!' she screamed into Nigel's ear, and then looked apologetically at the other parents and dragged him towards the front door looking for his father among the crowd.

That evening, Nigel was given no dinner and sent straight to his room. His father came to see him late that evening and sat silently across from him for a while. Nigel had never seen his father angry and wondered whether he would be now. His father seemed to have only one emotion: a cold indifference to anything that was going on around him. After staring at him for a while, his father shook his head and stood up. 'You embarrassed us today, Nigel. Don't ever do anything like that again.' With that, he walked out of the room, switching off the light on his way out. Nigel had been putting together a jigsaw puzzle, but now he could not see a thing. He began to cry.

A while later, just as he was about to fall asleep, his mother walked into his bedroom and turned on the light. 'Nigel, wake up. I have to talk to you.'

He sat up on his bed. He was still wearing the clothes he had worn to Jonah's party. His mother was always slightly more emotional than his father, but she kept a tight rein on her emotions for fear of upsetting his father, who believed that showing emotions, such as crying and shouting (and perhaps even smiling and laughing, in his case), was a sign of weakness.

'This behaviour...' His mother appeared to be trembling in an effort to keep a hold of her temper. 'It has to stop.'

'Sorry,' he heard himself say, even though he wasn't really sure why. If they had bought him toys, maybe he wouldn't want to play with other children's toys; he sizzled inside but made sure not to show it.

'You embarrassed us today,' she said, repeating what his father had said.

'But Mum...'

'Don't argue,' she said. 'Your father and I have brought you up to be a good boy. Why did you try to break Jonah's toy?'

'He wouldn't let me play with it,' said Nigel loudly, his lower lip protruding as he sulked.

'You have your own toys. That was *his* present.'

'I don't have any toys!'

'You have to learn to keep a hold of that temper, my boy. It's an ugly emotion. I won't have any son of mine behaving like that, do you hear me?'

Nigel felt as if his throat was tightening from the strangulating hold his parents had over his life. They controlled his every move, from what toys he could have, to with whom he could play.

'I hate you!' he said, standing up and pushing his mother, then bursting into tears.

11

'Say sorry, Nigel!' His father appeared at the door, as if from out of nowhere. His voice was loud. 'We won't have behaviour like that in this house.'

Nigel looked at his parents standing there emotionless, both of their faces set in miserable frowns that never changed from one day to the next, as if just breathing was a task. He remembered being at Jonah's party and seeing the way the other parents would laugh and joke with their children. He wanted parents like that. He remembered his cousin Jacoby shouting at his mother a few months ago. His aunt, Jacoby's mother, had told him not to shout at her, but then she had smiled and given him a hug and asked him what was wrong. Nigel could almost feel the warmth emanating from her. He couldn't understand why his parents were so different. It felt to him as if they didn't care about him.

He began to cry.

'You think about what you've done today, Nigel,' said his father harshly. 'Come on, Elena, leave him. He has to learn to behave like a decent human being, not like a brat. He's been spending too much time with your sisters' children, I think.'

Nigel hadn't seen his cousins for months. He missed them. They lived in normal, loving houses. His home was cold.

'That temper of yours has to go, young man,' said his mother. His parents turned out the light and closed the door behind them, leaving him standing in the middle of his room, tears pouring down his cheeks.

*

Wanting something to blame, Nigel began to wonder again, as he had done before, whether it was his parents' cold treatment of him that had caused him to hold so much anger inside him, and take that out on others. Or was he just inherently a bad person? Had they known what he would do one day, or had they started the chain of events that would lead to that fateful day? As he looked at the few bits of pasta that had now gone cold in his plate, he knew that no amount of blaming anyone else could get him out of this hole he had dug.

As a child and teenager, Nigel's angry temperament had been a backdrop to everything else in his life. It was almost obvious to most people in his life that, one day, it would be the unmaking of him. Most of his peers, however, were too afraid to say anything to him. His best friend, Mike, came from a similar background, and understood some of Nigel's reasons for feeling so resentful, but even he was worried for him.

One day, when Nigel and Mike were thirteen years old, a young boy who had recently joined their school made a comment about Nigel's hair whilst they were waiting in line at the school cafeteria at lunchtime. Nigel had begun to grow his hair as he was becoming a fan of Heavy Metal music, having heard a Led Zeppelin album at Mike's cousin's house.

'Your hair... I don't mean this in a bad way, but when I saw you from the back, I thought you were a girl,' scoffed the boy. Then, seeing Nigel's eyes narrow, he laughed as if to brush it off. 'It looks like my sister's hairstyle,' he added, the grin on his face showing that he thought it was quite a funny comment.

Nigel took a fork from the cutlery tray and stabbed the boy in the arm. Blood began to seep through the young boy's white cotton school shirt, and his face turned pale. Tears formed in his eyes. 'What did you do that for?' he yelled. 'I was only having a laugh.' By then, one of the girls had alerted a teacher, and Nigel looked up to see a very stern-faced Mr Jeffreys, his history teacher, who happened to be in the school canteen at the time.

'Price! It would have to be you, wouldn't it? What's wrong with you?'

'It was *his* fault,' said Mike, trying to defend his friend. 'He was making fun of him.' He pointed at Simon, the new boy, who was now crying and holding out his arm towards Mr Jeffreys.

'You come with me, Simon, we'll get you cleaned up,' he said, assessing the fork-marked scar on the boy's arm. 'I'll be talking to your parents, Nigel. Report to me for detention tonight!' With that, he walked away.

As he followed the teacher, Simon turned his head to face Nigel and stuck out his tongue.

As it turned out, Simon was in fact a real school bully, in a different league to Nigel altogether.

The next day, Simon and three of his friends, who were part of a gang called "The Tribe", followed Nigel and Mike on their way home. As they were walking through a park, Simon and his friends pounced on Nigel and gave him a beating that left him bleeding and bruised. If Mike hadn't run off for help, returning with two older boys who scared off the gang, Nigel may well have ended up in hospital—or worse.

Nigel didn't want to face his parents after the fight. It was not the first time he'd been in scrapes, although usually he was the perpetrator. He felt embarrassed. He asked Mike if he could go to his house to clean himself up before going home.

Nigel called his parents from Mike's house to tell them that he was doing his homework with Mike.

Later that evening, Mike and Nigel sat listening to music. Nigel was not very talkative.

'Are you okay, Nige?' asked Mike, concerned.

'Yeah, why wouldn't I be?'

'Er... you've just been beaten up by four thugs.'

'You just wait... I will get that Simon. He's too weak to fight his own battles, so he brings his stupid mates.'

'Didn't you hear what Roger said about Simon? His cousin goes to the school where Simon used to go. Apparently, he was expelled because he was going to stab a teacher.'

'That's just rumours.' Nigel scowled.

'It's not.'

'I'm not scared of Simon, okay?' Nigel walked over to the record player to change the record as it had finished. He lifted it off the turntable roughly, and threw it on the floor as he looked for another one to play.

'Hey! What are you doing? You'll could have broken that! Nige, you really have to do something about your temper.' Mike bent over and picked up the vinyl 7-inch single, checking it for damage.

'It's not broken.'

'I mean it,' said Mike, sitting back on the sofa. 'Sometimes, I feel like I don't really want to hang around with you because you always end up in fights, and I don't want to end up in a fight because of you.'

Nigel, who was now sitting on the floor next to the record player, looked up at Mike, red-faced. 'I was bloody beaten up! I was jumped on by a gang. I didn't start that!'

'You stabbed Simon with a fork yesterday. That's why they jumped you.'

'Huh! Simon should learn to fight his own battles. I am going to teach him that.' Nigel stood up. 'I'm going home.'

Mike stood up, too. 'I really think you should stay away from Simon. He's trouble.'

'What? So, I just let him get away with beating me up?'

'Nigel, if you say anything else to him, he'll beat you up again, and next time—'

Nigel sighed. 'Okay. I won't do anything.'

Mike breathed a sigh of relief.

Nigel felt angry with himself; the truth was, he was afraid. He had never before been challenged by anyone and had always managed to maintain his reputation as an undefeated bad boy. Simon had changed that. Luckily for Nigel, Simon's gang didn't trouble him again; they were the type to move from one victim to the next, leaving them battered and fearful. Nigel steered clear of Simon.

Throughout his youth, Nigel blamed his antisocial behaviour on his parents. He had unresolved anger towards them and their control of him, but felt unable to vent that except through aggression.

His parents ruled the home at a distance. They would act shocked or disappointed in him whenever he got angry and shouted at them, but never raised a hand to him in his formative years. The way they dealt with teaching discipline was to lock him away in his room for hours on end as a punishment after he had done something wrong or thrown a tantrum.

As soon as Nigel started to show his parents that he had interests outside the home over which they may not be able to have much control, their grip on him tightened even more. They thought of a new way to keep control.

One evening, when he was 14 years old, Nigel announced over dinner that he was going to a rock concert with Mike and Mike's cousin, Henry.

'You're too young for rock concerts,' said his mother.

'But Mike's going!'

'Mike's parents can decide whether their child goes to a rock concert or not. If they are not concerned about his welfare, that is their problem. We, however, do not think it is in your best interests to attend a rock concert.' His mother ate a spoonful of soup, as if to indicate that the discussion was over.

'Dad?' said Nigel.

'Eat your soup before it gets cold,' said his father, not meeting his eyes.

'I bet you were allowed to go to concerts when you were my age,' said Nigel, pouting.

'Life was different in our day,' said his mother. 'Young people today are unruly, out of control. Just look at the amount of fights you get into at school.'

'We should have sent him to a private school,' said his father.

'Dad, can I go to the concert?' pleaded Nigel. 'I promise I won't get into any trouble.'

'You heard your mother,' said his father, bringing a spoon of soup to his mouth.

Nigel hated his father at that moment, his stiff face with never a hint of a smile, never a tear from his eye. Always so controlled and so controlling. Nigel stood up and tipped his father's soup bowl upwards so that the steaming hot soup splashed over his shirt.

His father sat, eyes wide enough for the whites to be seen all around them, and a storm brewing on his face, as the red liquid from the tomato soup dripped down his blue tie. Nigel noticed how the light made the tie look purple where the soup had stained the blue fabric.

His mother stood up. 'Get up to your room, now!' she screamed.

The decibels were enough to send a shiver through Nigel, and he ran out of the kitchen, up to his room.

Later that evening, Nigel sat on his bed reading a book, having been locked in his room for over two hours. He heard the door unlock and thought he would now have to listen to a lecture from his father and then be told to go to bed. Instead, his father walked into the room, his eyes red around as if he had been crying. He was carrying a belt. 'Your mother and I cannot condone what you did earlier, Nigel. This temper of yours is getting out of hand. Do you know how embarrassing it is for us to be called into the headmaster's office every few weeks about something you've done? And now... now, you have shown your anger against your own parents.' He held up the thick, black leather belt. 'This will teach you a lesson that you won't forget.' Nigel had been whipped with his father's belt for the first time that night, but it wasn't the last.

***

In his late teens and twenties, Nigel began to drink, and this made his aggression even worse. Now, his uncontrolled anger was taken up a notch whenever he had a few too many.

Mike was the only friend he kept in touch with from his schooldays, having alienated many of the other pupils with his temper tantrums and frequent arguments and fights.

In their late teens, Mike and Nigel liked nothing better than to attend rock and heavy metal gigs. For Mike, it was something he was initiated into by his cousin Henry, a die-hard rock fan. Henry had posters of bands that covered every inch of his bedroom walls and he played the electric guitar almost as well as some of his idols. He had grown his hair longer than his sister's, something she said she found embarrassing, but Henry told Mike he suspected that she was just jealous of the lustre and shine of his hair compared to her own.

Henry had introduced Mike to heavy metal by taking him to a Deep Purple gig when he was barely in his teens. After that, Mike was hooked and began borrowing and playing Henry's records at home. Nigel soon became interested in this music that resonated with him; the heavy bass and drums, the melodic riffs, and the profound lyrics to which he could relate.

It wasn't long before Nigel caused a scene at a concert. He had been standing next to Mike, drinking and listening to the band when a young man—aged perhaps eighteen—pushed in front of them and began dancing to the music, swinging his arms around, banging his head, causing his hair to swing into Mike's face, and generally making a nuisance of himself. The other gig-goers in the vicinity moved aside and shook their heads, some even laughed at the man's crazy behaviour. Nigel, however, became enraged. This potent mixture of loud aggressive music and strong lager left him intolerant, and he swung his arms towards the man, causing the crowd who were looking on to take a sharp intake of breath. Nigel's punch landed the man on the floor. The man stood up after lying, disorientated, on the floor for a few moments. He then looked at Mike, whom he thought had thrown the punch. 'You bastard! Why did you do that?' He asked through gritted teeth.

'It wasn't...' Mike's voice drifted off. Such was his loyalty to Nigel, he was unable to continue.

Before he knew it, the man's fist was in his face, and blood squirted from Mike's mouth as a tooth was dislodged.

'That'll teach you, you wanker, you bastard,' slurred the man, obviously drunk. The man walked away, leaving Mike in shock.

Nigel was about to run after him, but Mike pulled him back. 'What the fuck are you doing?'

'I'm gonna get him,' said Nigel, trying to pull away from Mike's grip.

'No, you're not!'

Nigel looked on, incredulous. This was the first time Mike had ever ordered him to do anything. It was unexpected. He didn't know how to react.

They watched the rest of the show and returned home in complete silence. They never mentioned the incident, and Mike told his parents he had bitten into a hot dog that had a stone in it, to explain how he had dislodged a tooth. His father didn't believe him, Mike could tell by the look in his eyes. All he said was, 'That Nigel is a bad influence on you, son.'

And so it went on for much of their youth, Nigel getting into scrapes and Mike mostly trying to get them out of trouble. Nigel never did understand why Mike continued to stand by him as a friend, but he was genuinely grateful for that friendship; it was the only thing that kept him sane in an otherwise confusing and turbulent childhood.

Chapter 2

Nigel's breakdown happened quite suddenly and unexpectedly.

For months after the murder, he had tried to carry on as normal. He had made sure there was no evidence, nothing to link him to the crime. His clothes had been stained with the dead girl's blood, so he had called June from a public call box, telling her that there was a leaving do at work for one of the staff, and he would most likely be home late, after midnight. He knew that June never stayed up later than 11 p.m. It was like a clock existed inside her and she would switch off at exactly that time.

He arrived home at 11.30 p.m. and saw that all the lights in the house were turned off except the porch light—June had left that on for him. He had been sitting in his sweaty and stained clothes in his car for hours, and was worried that some of the blood may have rubbed off onto the car seat even though he had placed a plastic bag he'd found in the boot under him on the driver's seat.

Opening the front door of the house very slowly, not wanting to make any noise, he caught sight of his face in the hallway mirror and saw a dishevelled man staring back at him. His hair was windswept, parts of it stuck to his forehead as if with glue. He had suspicious brown marks on his chin and on the tip of his nose. *Blood?* Then he saw it, a scratch. As the girl had fallen to the ground after the hammer blow, she had reached up towards him, and her long fingernails had scratched his face from his cheekbone to his mouth. It was a fine line, but it was noticeable. Panic set in. How could he hide it? He remembered that June was always covering her facial spots with concealer... he would have to find that and use it. Could he pretend he'd cut himself shaving? He pondered that for an anxious moment but realised the scratch was too long for a razor cut.

Looking down at his clothing, he knew he would have to change as fast as possible and dispose of the clothes. He could not leave them in the laundry basket; they were covered with blood and grime. It was too late for him to turn on the washing machine. June might be awoken by the sound. He sighed and closed the front door behind him.

Once upstairs, he entered the bathroom, locked the door, and tore off his clothes in a frenzy. He wanted to wash away the night's events, leave them in the past, where they could disappear. He took a hot shower, almost burning his skin in his eagerness to remove any stain, any sign, any blemish. But he could not wash away what was already starting to grow inside him: a silent growl that would escalate and take over his mind in the days and weeks, months and years to come. A permanent reminder, tattooed in his brain.

When he was satisfied that he was clean, he took his soiled clothing and used the kitchen scissors to shred them into small pieces. When he was done, he felt as though he needed another shower. He didn't know if he was imagining it, but a smell, a stench, pervaded the area around him; a mixture of sweat, blood, fear, and the faint odour of a perfume or soap that had been worn by his victim. The odour was entrenched in his nose, and he felt afraid that it would stay with him always, no matter how hard he tried to clean up the mess.

He dumped the torn clothing into the bin outside the house. It was collection day tomorrow... it would be gone. He felt he could almost breathe again.

Even though he'd done the best he could to wipe the slate clean, the next day when he got into his car to go to work, he was shocked to see a brown line of dried blood on his window—at least, he thought it must be blood: it looked like blood. The events of the previous night flashed before him again.

Nigel was amazed at how he'd been able to go to work the next day, with all the turmoil going through his mind. He'd gone home after work and had dinner with his wife as usual. That night, he'd gone to bed and, surprisingly, had slept; he put that down to sheer exhaustion, as he'd not slept a wink the night of the murder. When he woke up the following day, he began to wonder whether he had actually dreamt the murder. The memory of the murder was somehow displaced. Had it really happened? Had he just been watching one of those cop shows that June loved so much, and fallen asleep and imagined he'd killed someone? It really seemed absurd when he thought about it. It couldn't have happened. *I wouldn't kill anyone.*

He'd never considered himself capable of murder. When he'd done it, when he'd watched her die, the regret was instant. He wanted to help her, but he knew that if he called the police, he would be locked up. It was a crime he had committed as if his body had been possessed. Looking back on it, he refused to believe he had done that, and for a while he almost succeeded in convincing himself that it had all been a dream.

Things changed when the news story made the national headlines. A young girl's body had been found: Emily Baxter. He now knew her name. When he looked at her photo in the newspaper, those same eyes looked back at him. In the photo, she was smiling, wearing a graduation robe. She'd been missing for two months, the news story said. A tear came to his eye.

June had shown him the newspaper as soon as he'd come home from work.

'Another young girl is murdered. What's the world coming to?' she said.

When she saw his reaction, the tears in his eyes, she smiled at him. 'You pretend you're a big, tough man, but you've got a real soft side, Nige, haven't you? I'm so glad we got married.' She kissed him on the lips. 'I love you,' she said softly, as dark thoughts invaded his mind.

His eyes had drifted down the page, and he read more about Emily Baxter. The pull was too great; although he tried to tear his eyes away, he could not. He knew he was hoping to read that she'd been a bad person, that he'd done the world a favour by getting rid of her. But the angelic photo of Emily was a fitting illustration for the news story. She was just an average girl. She hadn't deserved what he'd done.

As his eyes struggled to see through the increasing tears, he continued to read the story. When he thought things could not get any worse, he read the line: *"Miss Baxter was three months pregnant at the time of her death."*

Nigel hadn't known that. Would it have changed anything if he'd known? He wanted to believe it would have, but he doubted it. That fit of rage had turned him into someone he did not like, someone he did not recognise. Now he knew that he'd murdered two people that night. Emily *and* her unborn child.

Emily Baxter's body was washed onto the rocks by the tide not too long after she disappeared. It had lain hidden under some seaweed and other debris for a couple of months. Decomposing. An elderly man looking for coins with a metal detector had passed along that way and noticed what looked like a pile of rubbish beneath the stones and rocks. Thinking he might find some valuable items there, he'd pushed aside a rock and was instantly horrified by the sight that met his eye.

The skeletal body with straggly red hair was covered in dirt. He could make out the clothing and saw that it must have been a woman, once. The old man caught his breath and ran as fast as his legs could carry him to find the nearest phone and alert the police.

Bodies had been found on the beach here before; it was not that unusual at a cliff edge. Sometimes, it was swimmers who had gone in out of their depth; sometimes, it was accidental death; but more often, it was suicide.

Investigations were carried out to find out how old the deceased had been and to try to work out how many weeks or months the body had been decomposing. Research was done to try to reconstruct an image of what she would have looked like, her face long since gone from the bones of her skull. Missing persons records were looked into. A young girl, Yvonne Maidley, had gone missing a few weeks prior, and the local police immediately thought of her when the body was found, but this body turned out to be far too decomposed, and the deep red, russet hair colour did not fit with Yvonne's blonde hair.

The discovery of the body made local news first. Ameline Grace had been watching television with her parents when the news bulletin announced it. Ameline was ten years old.

'Mum, remember when we were driving by those cliffs after Miffy died and I saw the woman with the bright red hair fighting with that man? Do you think he threw her off the cliff? He looked really angry with her.'

'You have such a vivid imagination, Amy, darling.' Her mother laughed. 'Now, what do you want for tea?'

Ameline frowned and pouted. 'I'm being serious, Mum. The man looked straight at me, he was quite scary looking. The woman who died had red hair.'

'Hmm.' Ameline's father narrowed his eyes. 'Maybe she's onto something, Stacy. I remember there was a couple arguing by the side of the road. I didn't think anything of it at the time, but I did notice the red hair when we passed by and I had my full beams on. It was an unusual colour.'

'I don't remember seeing that.' Ameline's mother shook her head and shrugged.

'Dad, do you think we should tell the police?'

'It couldn't do any harm,' he replied. 'You're quite the amateur detective, aren't you, Amy?'

After hearing from the Grace family, the police launched an enquiry and made a plea for witnesses to come forward. It became national news.

* * *

Nigel sat next to June in their living room as the news came on.

"Police plea for witnesses to come forward after body found on beach."

A picture of the familiar rocky cliff edge and beach flashed onto the screen, and Nigel held his breath, feeling the sweat form on his forehead as the colour drained from his face.

"The body of a woman in her mid to late twenties was found on Chelsea beach on the morning of the 16th of October. A local man described the finding as 'hideous and grotesque; like something from a horror movie'. He had been using a metal detector along the cove when he came across the body. When the local news first aired exclusively on this channel, it resulted in witnesses coming forward. A ten-year-old girl and her father had witnessed an altercation between a man and woman on the 19th of August. The description they gave of the woman fitted that of the body on the beach. The family had been driving along Chelsea Cove when they saw a man arguing with a woman close to the cliff edge. Another local man described a similar couple and also gave a description of two cars at the scene, one of which police believe was later abandoned. The ten year-old witness has also given a very detailed description of the man to the police. Police are now looking for a man in his mid to late thirties with dark hair, of medium build. An E-FIT picture of the man is due to be published soon."

* * *

Emily Baxter's parents were watching the same news station. They sat in silence, both of them thinking the same thing but not wanting to say anything out loud. The 19th of August was the day Emily had disappeared. Emily had bright red hair.

A tear fell from Emily's mother's eye. She turned towards her husband. It had been over eight weeks since Emily disappeared, and she had not returned. It was the longest time she had ever stayed away without contact.

'I think we should go to the police,' said Emily's father, his face fixed in a sullen stare.

In the months following the news report, Nigel lived on a knife edge, always expecting the next phone call or the next knock on the door to be the police. The young girl had given a description of him to the police. The other witness had given descriptions of his and Emily Baxter's cars. Had that included number plates? Someone would be coming for him, he was sure of it.

Part of him was waiting, willing them to come, eager to get it over with. He'd done an unforgivable thing; he should pay his dues. Maybe then he would be able to sleep at night. But throughout this, he also felt fearful, afraid of being caught. He didn't really believe he was a murderer despite his subconscious mind nagging him constantly that he was. He kept telling himself he was acting in self-defence. *If I hadn't of killed her, she would have killed me, she had a gun; she was a mad woman.*

Somehow though, he kept going back to the fact that it was he who had lost his temper, who had got out of his car with a hammer and threatened her. She was a woman on her own. *She was the one acting in self-defence.*

The police were questioning her family, friends, neighbours, and colleagues about the murder. Emily had been living with her boyfriend, Russell Banks. According to a neighbour, who did not want to be identified, there had been an argument; he'd heard it through the wall. He said it was not unusual for Emily and Russell to argue. A couple of neighbours had seen Emily drive away. The description they gave of the car matched that of an abandoned vehicle found in a lay-by close to the scene.

Emily's family were not too concerned when she first went missing because she had left her boyfriend a few times in the past, after rows, and had gone to stay with friends, often not contacting them for weeks. It was not unusual for Emily. Her father described her as a very 'headstrong and streetwise' girl. He said she could look after herself, so they'd not been worried.

Nigel read the words: *"She could look after herself"* in a news story, and recalled the altercation they'd had before he'd dealt the blow that killed her. She had certainly been a tough girl. She had riled him with her words... made him angry. There it was again, that word: *angry*. Anger. He was afraid of that emotion. He wondered whether there was a phobia called angryphobia because he now lived as if he were walking on eggshells, afraid, and fearful that he would fall into that uncontrollable state again and... the consequences did not bear thinking about.

Through questioning Emily's closest friends, the police discovered that she had been having an affair with a man who lived about three miles from her. The man, Ramiro Lopez, was pictured in the paper alongside a picture of Emily's long-term boyfriend. Both men were now suspects.

Nigel read the descriptions of the men and remembered Emily saying that her boyfriend was a boxer; he wondered which one of these men was the boxer. If only he'd got into the car and been driven away by Emily to meet his fate at the hands of either Ramiro or Russell, he would now be dead. He wished he was. It would be easier than this.

The months that followed continued to shed light on Emily's life and her background. Nigel was learning more and more about this girl he had killed. He knew where she was born, how old she was, that she had two sisters, and that she was working for the local council at the time of her death. He also learnt how, as a child, Emily had suffered from a heart condition that meant she was in and out of hospital. She'd had a successful operation to cure the condition as a teenager, and due to her many trips to hospital, had developed a desire to help others. During her time as a student, she had done voluntary work at the local NHS hospital. So many of the news reports described her as 'caring', and 'kind'. All of this only served to nauseate Nigel and create more of a burden for him. When she'd stood up to him that night, and when she'd held a gun up to him, he'd imagined she must be some kind of criminal. Killing her would never be an easy burden to bear, but thinking that she was someone who'd been willing to kill him had made it easier to deal with. Now, here, the evidence stood before him in black and white that she was a good person. She was probably frightened of him which is why she'd threatened him. Still, he had to find a way to live with himself, so he told himself that she had a gun... that was illegal, surely? She could not be the angel or saint that the newspapers were making her out to be. But his guilt remained; he had no escape. She was dead and no matter who she was, he had killed a person. He was a murderer.

June would talk about Emily when Nigel returned from work. It felt to him that this was all she would ever talk about. 'Isn't it sad about that girl, Emily? I hope they find out who murdered her. She was a good person... I feel sorry for her family. Did you know, they're saying she was three months pregnant when she died. Do you think it could have been an accident? She'd had an argument with her boyfriend that night. Do you think she killed herself? She was having an affair... maybe her boyfriend found out.'

June's relentless commentary about the latest findings in Emily Baxter's case added to Nigel's pent-up anxiety. He wanted to shut her up, stop her talking. Sometimes, he found himself imagining doing the same thing to her as he had done to Emily. At those times, he would freeze and his mind would seize up as if he was trying to stop himself thinking. He remembered hearing somewhere that the first murder is the worst one; after that, some murderers get a taste for it. After the first one it's easy. That's why there are so many serial killers. *But I'm not a murderer,* he would argue with his conscience.

Up until that day, Nigel had been what he considered *ordinary*. He knew he was a bit short-tempered, but he lived and worked around people who also had a short fuse. It was stress, he used to tell himself; the pace of life in modern times. Whenever he'd had an argument with June and made her cry in the past, he'd put it down to stress or on having a bit too much to drink. Alcohol was one of his weaknesses. But he hadn't even been drinking on the evening in question.

That night lived with him, followed him, owned him. He had the date imprinted on his mind, the 19th of August 1991. In fact, he could remember every single detail about that day, as he had gone over it and over it so many times, trying to find out if there was a reason... something to blame it on. Twenty years later, he still hadn't found one.

He could remember what he was wearing, who he'd seen, what he'd talked about. It was as if there was a map of his life and that day was highlighted on the map; every single detail preserved.

Chapter 3

19th August 1991

Nigel's alarm clock sounded at 7.30 a.m. He yawned and stretched his arms above his head. His head felt heavy.

June moved slightly in the bed beside him. They'd had an awful row the night before because he'd left the front door open when he got home from the pub and had gone straight to bed. June had got up to go to the toilet at midnight and heard some voices outside. Walking down the stairs, she'd noticed the door wide open and a group of young boys across the road. They could have easily got into the house and stolen things, or worse.

June stormed up the stairs and woke Nigel. She'd screamed at him, 'It's not the first time you've done that! Why do you insist on going out and getting so drunk that you leave your brain in the pub?'

'Oh, shut up! I have to get up for work in the morning. Anyone can accidentally leave a door open.'

'No... No, actually. I've never forgotten to close the front door and I don't think I know anyone else who has. Do you know how many crimes have been committed in this neighbourhood recently? Anyone could have got in.'

'But they didn't! Would you just shut up, woman! I have to get some sleep.'

'You're turning into an old drunk. It won't be long before you start forgetting where you live and end up sleeping on the streets.'

'It would be better than sleeping here. I'd probably get more peace. Don't you ever stop talking?'

'I'm telling you, Nigel, you have got to start behaving your age or I'm leaving you. I don't want to be married to an old drunk. When you're in your fifties, you'll be incoherent and an alcoholic.'

*

Nigel thought back to that day. He was in his fifties now, and June wasn't too far wrong in her prediction. He wasn't an alcoholic; the killing had put an end to his drinking binges, as he always felt that he had to be in control of his temper as much as possible. But he was incoherent. His power of speech seemed to be leaving him slowly, as if he no longer felt worthy enough to say anything.

The day of the 19th of August 1991 had been an endless sequence of complaints. One of the worst days he'd had working for the company. It was almost as if the technology had turned against him. Computers could work out a lot of things, but they could not have made a prediction that he would kill someone; it couldn't have been that. Many times over the years, he wondered about the law of karma. So many things had gone wrong for him that day. Was that the reason he had been so over-aggravated that he'd ended up killing, or had the universe conspired to make the worst kind of day so that he would forever be looking back on it and reliving it? A kind of cosmic payback for the murder. "If there's going to be a day he'll have to remember for the rest of his life, let's make it the worst ever memory. He deserves it, the murdering brute," the gods of revenge seemed to be saying.

Every time Nigel remembered the murder—which was every waking moment (and every sleeping moment because of the frequent nightmares)—he would go over the events of that day. He was constantly reliving the worst day of his life. *Surely this is purgatory*, he reasoned.

He'd been offered help after his breakdown. His GP wanted to refer him to counselling with a psychologist. But Nigel resisted. He had an inbuilt fear since the murder that anyone who looked at him would be able to see the guilt written on his face. Surely those trained to read signs of body language, to fathom what a person was thinking, would be able to tell that he was a murderer; a cold-blooded killer who had slain a stranger in a random act of violence committed in anger. Undeserved. A pregnant woman. A life inside her ended before it could even begin.

Many of his nightmares involved a crying baby and a mother with rage in her eyes, screaming at him, trying to make the child stop crying. Emily Baxter's eyes. Brown. Large. Shocked.

A few days after he'd found out that Emily had been pregnant when he killed her, June announced *she* was pregnant. She was over the moon. 'I know we didn't plan it, but we've talked about starting a family. I've always wanted children,' she cooed.

'But... but... we can't afford a child.' His mind was racing. *What am I saying? Am I asking her to have an abortion? Isn't abortion murder? I've already killed one child. But how can we have a child? Emily Baxter's child never had the chance to live because of me. Emily never had the chance to be a mother, how can I be a father?*

The anxiety was clear on his face.

'Nige.' June hugged him. 'Don't worry. We can afford it. I've been putting some money aside every month.'

'You've been planning to have a baby?' He almost screamed that, as if she were the one who'd murdered Emily, as if she were the one who didn't deserve to have a child. But then he caught himself. The anger. He had to keep the anger at bay. The anger was what had caused him to kill. He'd seen advice about anger management on television; take a deep breath, count to ten slowly.

In his mind, he began... *one... two... three...*

'I wasn't planning a child,' June said, obviously dejected by his statement and the tone in which he'd delivered it. He could see it in her eyes: *Why isn't he happy? Doesn't he want to have children with me?*

Nigel sighed and said in a small voice, the voice that had started to replace the more confident one he'd used for most of his life: 'I'm sorry, I shouldn't have shouted.'

'I know it's come as a bit of a shock,' said a now subdued June as she stared at her hands. 'But I just know we'll be great parents.' She looked up at him tentatively.

He forced a smile.

Murderer. The voice nagged again. The constant repetitive voice that talked to him all the time. The voice in his head. *Murderer. Murderer. Murderer.* It was ever present, it never left. Like a heartbeat or a breath, it continued. It was there when he woke up; it was there when he stirred his tea in the morning; it was there keeping time with the chugging train on his way to and from work. Even twenty years later, it was still there.

When June was three months pregnant, they sat together one evening, watching a soap opera. When it ended she began: 'Remember that woman that was murdered? Emily Baxter?' Her eyes met his and he tensed.

What had happened? What was she about to tell him? Was she going to ask him to confess? Was she going to mention something about that night? Had she put the pieces of the jagged puzzle together and worked out that she was married to a murderer?

Paranoia swept through his mind. He could not speak, and his eyes could not avoid the pull of her gaze. Part of him was hoping that she knew, so that this living nightmare would be over. He could be arrested, thrown behind bars, punished. *I should be punished. Maybe by being punished, by being able to talk about it, maybe that would bring some relief?*

But she went on to say, 'The police have let her boyfriend go, for now. He'd been at work on the evening she disappeared, and more than three of his work mates spoke up for him. He could still be called back for questioning at a later date, though, because no one really knows for sure *when* Emily was killed. It could have been the night she disappeared, or it could have been later. The man she was having an affair with is still a suspect, too.'

Why does she keep talking about this case? Nigel's mind whirred. Was it because of their close proximity? He remembered once, as a child, he had read his best friend's mind. They had been sitting next to each other watching TV and he'd heard Mike say, 'This programme is rubbish'.

Nigel had replied, 'That's what I was thinking,' and had stood up to turn over the channel.

Mike said, 'What?'

'I just agreed with you. You said this programme is rubbish. I was going to switch over.'

'I didn't say anything,' said Mike, frowning.

'He didn't say anything,' said Mike's mother who was sitting on the other side of the room, knitting.

Wide-eyed, Mike looked at him and said: 'I did think it, though.'

Maybe that's what's happening with June? he thought. They were so close to each other every day they might be able to read each other's thoughts... Could she tell that he was thinking about this case all the time? He took a deep breath and tried to stop his overactive imagination. After all, the case was on the news daily, and June wasn't the only person who was talking about it. Everyone was. At work, he'd overheard people trying to guess what had happened. There was nowhere he could go to avoid the chatter, and even when he was out of earshot of all the gossips and amateur detectives, his conscience continued to assault him: *Murderer. Murderer. Murderer.*

Nigel and June celebrated the birth of their baby daughter, Annabelle, on the 12th of May 1992. Well, June celebrated. Nigel felt unworthy. When he looked at the angelic baby in his arms, all he could remember was how he had caused the death of something so innocent, so tiny, so helpless. Emily Baxter's baby never had a chance to live.

It was not too long after Annabelle was born that Nigel had his breakdown.

When his breakdown finally came it was something of a relief. It had been a slow-brewing storm. One day, he found himself in the car park of his local *Sainsbury's*, holding two bags of shopping and not knowing why he was there, where his car was, whether he even owned a car, or where he lived. He knew his name was Nigel, but when he said it out loud, it sounded almost foreign. *Is that really my name?* he questioned himself.

He remained standing there as people rushed past to get to their cars. He tried to work out how he had got there. He couldn't remember driving to the shop or buying anything. Somehow though, something inside him was telling him that he should not drive, he should take a train, not drive—it was too dangerous. But he couldn't understand why he was thinking that.

He looked in the shopping bags as if they would hold clues to his identity and why he had come. He found a packet of nappies for a newborn. *But I don't have a baby*, he thought. He dropped the bags and heard the sound of a bottle breaking. Soon, red wine was pouring under his feet. He stood stock still, not noticing or even caring. He was still wondering why he was there and where he was supposed to be going next.

Without thinking, he sat down on the ground; sat on the red wine puddle. Then, he took off his shoes and started laughing very loudly at what he'd done, but even though he was laughing, he couldn't work out why. He kept thinking, *I should be walking, I should be walking*. Finally, he stood up and began to walk.

The faces of puzzled shoppers watched him walk by. Whispers buzzed around him, and hands pointed to the bags he had left on the ground. He had stopped laughing. He was scowling now as he looked around at the people watching him. They turned away.

He continued to walk and then reached a main road. He felt as though someone had reached inside of him and grabbed hold of his heart, giving it a sharp tug. His breathing became shallow, and he struggled for air. He began to scream, overwhelmed by fear. 'Help me! Help me!' he called out as people walked by. Some looked at his trousers, noticing the red wine that had stained the brown corduroy. He heard a woman ask her companion: 'Is that blood, do you think?'

'He smelt of alcohol; he must be drunk,' her friend replied.

Nigel had not been shouting 'Help me' aloud, it had just been in his head, as had the sensation of him having a heart attack. He was now standing there on the kerb, no shoes on.

He stood in the same place for hours, thinking he was calling for help but to no avail, watching people walk past him as if he were invisible, the odd person commenting on his attire to a friend as they walked by. Eventually, he collapsed.

He was taken to hospital and told he'd had some kind of an "episode", but no one seemed to know anything.

He was taken to see a psychiatrist. He sat and nodded at the questions, shaking his head when necessary. He had by now remembered his name; in fact, he now recalled most things about his life, or so he thought. He wished he hadn't remembered the murder... he would be better off forgetting. He told himself that maybe he was imagining that he'd been involved in a murder, after all, his mind was not well. Something was wrong. Nervously, he shrugged off all the psychiatrist's concerns, saying he'd been having to deal with a lot of stress at work and with a new baby on the way. The psychiatrist narrowed her eyes at that comment: 'But you already have a three-month-old baby, Mr. Price. Is your wife pregnant again?'

'Er... no.' Not so distant recollections of a baby crying and waking him up began to fill his mind. That part of his memory had been buried and he had to dig to find it. 'I'm sorry,' he said to the psychiatrist. 'What I meant to say was it's stressful having a newborn baby and working.'

'Yes, yes it is,' she nodded. 'You may have had something like a nervous breakdown, Mr. Price. Are you sure you don't have any other weighty issues on your mind? Have you been losing sleep? You do look tired.'

'Um.' Nigel fiddled with his thumbnail as he spoke, head down. 'As I said, the baby wakes me up and I have to go to work.' He raised his head to look her in the eye, forcing a smile. 'I have a long commute and I think it will take me some time to get used to the change. Do you have children?'

'I know what it's like to have to look after a baby and balance work life.' The psychiatrist looked at him through narrowed eyes, as if she were still concerned but could not really pinpoint what his problem could be. 'I'll have a word with the consultant here. I don't think it's necessary to keep you in, but I might prescribe an antidepressant of some sort... or an anti-anxiety drug. I'll need to check what other medication you're on. Maybe you should also look into counselling. I will suggest that to your GP, so he can refer you somewhere. Mr. Price.' She took off her glasses and looked him in the eye, causing him to want to look away, but he thought he should retain eye contact to show that he had nothing to hide. 'These types of episodes can be indicators of other medical problems. You shouldn't ignore any other symptoms, but should go straight to your GP.' With a look of concern, she stood up and walked out of the room.

Nigel was released from hospital later that day, with a blot on his medical records questioning his sanity. He felt relieved that he had been let out—and afraid at how he had so easily lost control of his mind. It was similar to how he had lost control of his temper when he killed Emily. He felt cold inside, as if somehow his life was not his own anymore; he was like a puppet on a string, acting in ways that shocked him. He knew he had to sort it out somehow, but would not agree to any psychotherapy, for fear of being discovered as a murderer. He was aware that something wasn't right and without help he was heading down a slippery slope, but he reasoned that it would be easier if he lost his mind completely, rather than find it again and have to face up to what he had done.

The next few months were hard as he tried to resist any help offered by his GP, and he found his life with June suffering even more because of it. She had noticed his sour and silent moods and could not understand why he did not want to be treated. She had offered to go with him to the psychologist for counselling. She tried to make him take the antidepressants, but he refused everything. He feared what the medication could do to his senses... would he be able to keep as tight a grip on all the lies if he was under the influence of a drug? He'd heard of people telling all their secrets to doctors when they were given sedatives for operations. He could not risk his tongue betraying him. He slipped further and further from reality as he found himself cocooned in a world of his own with as little human contact as possible. Fear became his only friend. He deliberately steered away from people, not wanting them to find out what he had done. Surely, it was only a matter of time before the chanting in his head would find its way to his vocal chords? *Murderer, murderer, murderer...*

Chapter 4

On the night he killed Emily Baxter, Nigel had screamed at her, 'You nearly killed me, you bitch!'

Her car had come to a sudden halt at a set of traffic lights. Nigel had been driving fast, above the speed limit, Suicidal Tendencies' *How Will I Laugh Tomorrow...* blaring from his car speakers as he sang along loudly. He'd seen the amber light up ahead as he approached and even saw Emily's car in front of his, but he put his foot down on the accelerator, determined to get through the lights. Emily had put her foot on the brakes, seeing the amber light as she approached. This forced Nigel to brake suddenly to avoid rear-ending her car, and he had skidded to the side of the road. They were driving on a road that ran along a cliff edge. If he had skidded just a few more metres, he would have gone over the edge.

Many times over the years, since the murder, Nigel had imagined his car hurtling over that cliff edge. He could feel the freedom of it, cursing his luck: dying that night would have saved him from his torment and his ongoing battle to stay sane. What a relief it would have been, what a perfect ending. He often fantasised about it, like someone would fantasise about taking the ideal holiday or buying a dream home. He was almost willing time to reverse, to go backwards, back to that day... He had it all planned out; he would press hard on the accelerator when he reached that dangerous curve of the cliff edge. But no matter how hard he tried to imagine it, it buzzed around in his mind like a wasp trying to escape to the outdoors through a solid pane of glass. He could not turn back the clock, could not change his past.

'You nearly killed me', he'd screamed. *If only you had killed me, Emily... if only you had killed me.*

That evening, it had been raining, but he'd got out of his car. Theirs were the only two cars on that road. It was off the beaten track; one of those roads only used as a short cut by locals, or a way to avoid traffic. But in this type of weather, it was treacherous, unforgiving, and most local drivers avoided it, aware of the number of fatalities reported on the news each month. It was a twisting road, one not for the faint-hearted; there were hardly enough lights to see the road ahead clearly. Driving on that road in the dark *and* in the rain was almost like playing Russian roulette, taking your life in your hands, driving with a blindfold. The local council had begun to fit some cats' eyes on the road, and these works had been ongoing since the last major accident where three cars collided and sent a lorry toppling off the cliff edge into the sea, killing the driver instantly, and causing locals to petition for a safer road. It was often people who were not from the area who would use this road after getting lost whilst driving, and they would frequently end up in the local A&E.

Nigel mostly took the main road on his way home from work, but sometimes he preferred to avoid the queues of traffic. He knew this road quite well and was aware that he drove too fast on it. His speed reflected his confidence. But even so, he'd often felt guilty about speeding along the road when he arrived home and heard about the latest person to lose his or her life on it.

Emily was not a local; she'd strayed onto the cliff road, her car making unsteady progress along the potholed surface. Before the incident with Nigel, she had been thinking of turning around and going back to the main road, fearing for her safety whenever she reached a particularly hazardous part of the road nearing the cliff edge. Her hesitancy at the traffic lights was due to the fact that she was unfamiliar with the road. She'd preferred to play safe and slow down. She had no idea that Nigel's car was racing up behind her, hell bent on beating the lights.

In some ways, whenever Nigel thought back to that night, he believed that he, too, had lost his life on that road.

Chapter 5

19th August 1991

The traffic light still red, Nigel jumped out of the car, leaving the door hanging open, his music blaring into the night air. He flicked open the boot and grabbed his hammer from the toolbox; he couldn't be too sure who was in the car, so he wanted protection.

Anger swelled his chest and he was spurred on by the intro to the Metallica tune, *No Remorse*, that was now playing on his cassette. His heart beat fast and his temples throbbed. He had almost swerved over the cliff edge because he'd had to do an emergency stop to avoid ramming the car in front. That driver had some explaining to do!

When he approached the car window, he saw a woman in the driver's seat, and his temper flared even more. 'Typical!' he said out loud. 'A fucking woman driver!'

He'd always thought that women shouldn't drive. They were too unstable, in his opinion, always hormonal either with PMS or some other neurotic complaint. Whenever he was in the car with his wife driving, he told her he feared for his life.

Just last week, she had driven him to work when his car broke down, and he'd told her it was the last time he was ever getting into a car with her again.

'You're such a male chauvinist at times, Nige! Can you hear yourself?' said June.

'I'm only speaking the truth, and the truth can hurt. I don't feel safe when you're driving. If women didn't drive, there would be no car accidents,' he said, opening the car door to get out.

She burst out laughing. 'Um... actually it's teenage boys who cause the most traffic accidents.'

41

'You're listening to hearsay and gossip,' he said, turning to look at her. 'Men drive better than women because we can deal with speed better. It's all about perception. When things go too fast, women can't keep up. Your brains are smaller—'

'Er... no, actually I've heard they shrink to the size of a man's when we're pregnant.' She giggled.

'Oh, where did you read that? In a women's magazine? The proof is plain to see. Women can't park. When was the last time you saw a man struggling to get into a parking space?'

'Plenty of men can't park—'

'I see it every day,' interrupted Nigel, 'some poor woman trying to squeeze her Mini into a gap where a lorry would fit quite comfortably.'

She laughed. 'Women are the least likely to have an accident, actually.'

'Where did you hear that? Oh, come on, June. My evidence is from meatier publications. I read quality newspapers, not tabloids and girlie magazines. That's another thing: you women are such lightweights when it comes to reading. Your brains can't take in too much information. Look at how few women go into politics.'

'Er... maybe that's because it's boring. And anyway, there are lots of women in politics. In case you've forgotten, our last prime minister was a woman.'

'No, I haven't forgotten. Look what a mess she left us in,' he said. 'Women are just not cut out for those types of jobs.'

'Lots of women go into all sorts of jobs: doctors, lawyers, accountants, teachers...'

'Huh, women only go into those jobs until they fall pregnant. Face it, June, women have babies. It's nature's way of telling you to stay at home and look after the kids.'

'You're starting to annoy me now, Nige. You're such a dickhead at times. Get out of my car.'

Nigel glared at the woman in the driver's seat. She rolled down the window and looked a bit less confident when she noticed the hammer in his hand.

'What the fuck was all that about?' he growled.

'What do you mean?' she said, shrugging.

Now she was really starting to try his patience. She'd just caused him to do an emergency stop, a dangerous move on this hazardous road, and she was acting as if she was oblivious.

'You nearly killed me, you bitch!'

'Oh, go and sober up!' she shouted, reaching down to wind up the window.

Nigel smashed the glass before he even had time to think about what he was doing. It shattered into tiny pieces. 'Get out of the car!'

'No, you lunatic! I won't.'

He heard her engine revving as she got ready to take off at the lights. He jumped in front of her car to stop her. She began to hoot the horn.

Nigel looked around him anxiously, but relaxed when he saw there was no one around. Feeling more confident, he smashed the windscreen with the hammer; that would teach her. He watched as droplets of glass showered over her.

'You bastard!' Jumping out of the car, surprising him with her agility, she opened the car boot and took out a pistol. 'Drop the hammer, you fucking pisshead,' she screamed, pointing the pistol at him.

'You wouldn't dare,' he said, a bit less confidently.

'Try me. I've got the law behind me, even if I do kill you. I'm a woman, you're a madman who has threatened me. It's self-defence, you bastard. I'd enjoy watching you die.'

Despite her loud words and threats, he could see her arm shaking, and she appeared to be trembling. *She's just scared*, he thought. *She wouldn't shoot.* But something in her eyes told him he could not count on that.

He found himself wishing another car would arrive; this woman was like a loose cannon. He put his hands up in the air. 'I'm going back to my car,' he said.

He watched as she turned and kept the gun aimed at him. As he neared his car he could hear *Medusa* by Anthrax playing on his car stereo. He almost laughed at the irony. But he could not shake the fear he felt.

'And, tell Russ he can rot in hell,' she shouted.

'Who's Russ?' he asked, confused.

She looked at him through nervous eyes, as if sizing him up to work out if he was being sincere. She definitely seemed unhinged in some way.

He sat in his car, looked up, and saw the woman put the gun back into the boot of her car and walk around to the driver's side.

That was when the anger resurfaced and took over. How dare she threaten him like that? Bitch! She was the one who'd nearly killed him with her careless driving. And she can't be all that innocent if she's got a gun! He stormed back towards her and grabbed her arm before she had a chance to get into her car.

'You won't get away with threatening me like that!' he shouted.

'Why? Because you're such a big man and I'm just a little woman? I know your type. You're not secure in your masculinity, so you have to pick on someone smaller than you. What would you have done if I was a six-foot body builder? Huh?' Her voice was high-pitched and grating. She sneered at him.

She reached for the hammer in his hand, and he pulled hard to stop her taking it. She refused to give up.

A car drove past them, distracting Nigel for a moment. This was the first car he'd noticed since he'd stopped... He racked his brain trying to remember if there had been others. Would someone notice the commotion and alert the police?

The car's horn beeped as it went by. Nigel looked into the car and saw an elderly gentleman who appeared to be annoyed that they were blocking his way, making it necessary for him to overtake and drive on the wrong side of the road. The road was only wide enough for two medium sized cars to travel along it comfortably. The man seemed oblivious to their altercation. At least, Nigel hoped so.

While Nigel was distracted by the car, lost in thoughts of being arrested for threatening behaviour and criminal damage... he had loosened his grip on the hammer. The woman was now holding it.

'Let's see if you're such a big man now, without your weapon, shall we?' She narrowed her eyes with an evil glare.

'Bitch!' he retorted.

'By the way, you're paying for the damage to my car. My boyfriend used to be an amateur boxer. He was undefeated. He won't take kindly to this.' She waved a hand at the broken windows. 'Get in!' she ordered as she ran around to the boot and retrieved the gun. 'Go on! Get in! You're coming with me. We're going to see what my boyfriend makes of all this. Oh, and maybe the police.' She held the gun towards him.

'Huh! Police.' He quivered as he said it, fear embracing him. 'If you're such a law-abiding citizen, how come you've got a gun?'

'Get in the car before I shoot you.'

'You don't have the guts,' he said, his voice shaking at the last word, as he stood staring into her wild brown eyes, the gun hovering just in view.

'You're a fucking coward, you freak!'

'Give me my hammer back. I'm going home; I've had enough of you.'

'No! You're fucking coming with me, you loser. Get in the bloody car!' Her voice was loud and her demeanour intimidating, as if she had grown a few inches through her anger.

45

Nigel felt himself tremble. 'Y... You can't drive that, it's got shattered glass all over the place.'

'And whose fault is that?' She gave him a searing look, waving the gun dangerously close to him.

Another car drove past. She had anticipated that, having heard the vehicle approach, and lowered the weapon out of view, her eyes still fixed on him, like a lioness guarding her prey.

Nigel caught a glimpse of a young girl in the back of the car and a man and woman in the front; her parents, presumably. The couple looked as though they were having a heated conversation, although again, the driver took a moment to beep his horn as he drove past indicating annoyance at having to swerve to avoid the stationary vehicles.

Nigel saw his chance to grab the hammer from the woman, while she was distracted watching the rear headlights of the car disappear around the bend. He reached and pulled it from her hand with a sharp tug, causing her to fall backwards. She dropped the pistol, and he scrambled to get it before she could reach it.

'Not such a smart arse now you have no weapons, are you?' he gloated, holding up the hammer and gun as if they were trophies.

She lifted herself off the ground, slowly, keeping a safe distance between them, obviously wary of him. Her eyes darted around as if she were looking for someone to help out. 'I need that pistol back. It's not mine... my boyfriend is looking after it for a friend... He's in a gang. Please...'

Fear caused her to tremble.

Nigel put the pistol in his jacket pocket.

'Give it back, you freak!' She lunged towards him and reached into his pocket.

He pushed her away, but she resisted. He wouldn't let her have the weapons again; she seemed unhinged. 'Get lost, you bitch!' He pushed her forcibly, and she fell onto the ground.

Looking back at her, he shook his head and walked towards his car. He could hear the guitar solo from *Infinite Dreams* by Iron Maiden, and quickened his pace wanting to get back to the relative normality of his life before this weird woman invaded his peace. Then he felt a push from behind and fell forward. Managing to keep his balance and not fall to the ground, he instinctively turned around and saw her standing there. She grabbed his arm, and again tried to reach into his jacket pocket.

'Are you mad or something? Do you really think I'd give you the gun back?' he yelled, pushing her away. He held his hammer towards her. 'Keep away from me, you she-devil. You nearly killed me tonight. I could have gone over the cliff edge because of your careless driving.' He began to remember the reason why he had got out of his car to confront her in the first place.

'If you were a better driver, you'd have been looking where you were going!' she retorted angrily. 'Just give me the gun back and I'll let you go, okay?'

'Let me go? What the fuck are you talking about?' Who was this woman, thinking she had the right to tell him where he could be... *Let me go? What the hell is she talking about?* 'I'm going, and I'm taking the gun with me,' he growled, irate at her nerve.

She pounced on him, the anger from her dark eyes piercing through him. She grabbed at his jacket pocket. He swung his hand that held the hammer, and it caught the back of her head. For a brief moment, he felt satisfaction: he'd stopped her. *That'll teach her!* But then her eyes widened in shock. Her wide brown eyes glazed over as she stared at him, although she appeared to be unable to focus. Then, slowly, she fell onto the ground, at his feet, unconscious.

47

He began to breathe quickly, unsure what to do. His mind now tuned into everything around him, and he heard the music playing in his car. The chorus of Motörhead's *Killed by Death* mocked him as he caught sight of a trail of blood now creating a pool behind her red hair as it merged with rain water. He almost felt like laughing, but then the gravity of the situation presented itself. This wasn't a joke. *She might be de...* He couldn't bear to think of it. Those eyes still stared. He ran to his car and switched off the car stereo, angrily, wiping sweat from his brow.

His breath came quickly, in short pants. It was terrifying, almost as if he would choke before he could catch the next breath. *Calm down, calm down, you're just panicking, it'll be okay*, he tried to convince himself. *She might be all right.*

Thoughts whizzed through his head at lightning speed, too fast for him to make any sense out of them. If he called the police, he knew they would ask too many questions, he would be found out... especially if she survived and spoke up. She'd said her boyfriend was a boxer; he'd make mincemeat out of him. Nigel had never been interested in sports. Now in his mid thirties, he was skinny, weak looking; nerd like. He'd have no chance against this woman's irate boyfriend. The only thing he could think of was that he had to get away. Maybe she would be okay and someone would come along and find her, call an ambulance...

By the time she had time to report anything he could be long gone; he'd leave town, change his name, go into hiding. He could lie to June, tell her he'd been relocated for work, tell her that he'd always hated the name Nigel Price and had always wanted to be called Rocky Balboa or something; he laughed to himself, almost hysterically, at the way his thoughts were leading him down absurd paths, avoiding the one thing that his eyes would not depart from: his stare was fixed on the blood pooling around the girl, who lay prone on the ground, unmoving. Her eyes had been looking ahead like that for such a long time... There was no way she could still be alive. He shivered uncontrollably as the adrenaline coursed through him.

As he began to turn the key in the ignition, ready to leave, he noticed the bloody hammer lying on the ground under her head. It was sticking out behind her neck, with blood glistening on the silver head, caught in the moonlight at just the right angle. Evidence. His fingerprints were all over the hammer. Although he'd never been in trouble before... The police didn't have his prints... But what if the case was reopened in the future and what if the police had his fingerprints then? It was possible that the law would change so that everyone had to have fingerprints kept on record. His mind felt like it would explode with all the worry and fear. He knew he had to retrieve the hammer. He couldn't leave it there.

Getting out of the car slowly, he looked around him. If another car drove by now, he would be caught, especially if seen trying to get the hammer. He jumped back into his car, heart pounding. As he sat in his seat, he felt the heavy weight of the pistol in his jacket pocket against his chest. A gasp emanated from his mouth. *I can't keep it.* He knew that if anyone found it in his possession, it would be something to link him to her. What if she had a licence for it? It seemed odd, but it was possible, wasn't it? He had no clue how the licence laws for guns worked. But then he remembered her saying that her boyfriend was holding the gun for a gang member. That thought caused his chest to burn with even more dread. What if it was found on him and somehow this gang found him? God only knew what they would do to him.

With that thought nagging at him, he leapt out of his car and to the edge of the cliff. The vast sea beckoned. For a split second, he saw it as a way out of this mess, but shook the thought away. He reached into his jacket pocket and threw the gun as far away as he could. He tried to see where it had fallen, but it was starting to get very dark now. He had no idea whether it had actually made it to the sea at all, and even if it had, what if it was washed onto the shore by the tide? Someone might find it and trace the owner...

He tried to stop his overactive brain. All his fingerprints would be gone by the time it was found, anyway. If he could just do the same with the hammer, he would be home free.

As he turned back towards the road, guilt swooped down upon him; there she was, lying down, dead probably, because of him. He had killed her, and there he was, trying to find ways to save himself. He began to cry at the futility of it. He could not change what had happened: he had to do the best he could. He thought of driving to the nearest police station, handing himself in. That would be the right thing to do, but as his chest rose and fell with his sobs, he knew he could not do it. He was a good person, he told himself... this was a mistake, it shouldn't have happened, he hadn't meant to kill her... she had been shouting at him, winding him up. It was *her*... she was to blame... he didn't usually do things like this. Unable to understand what his feelings were, battling with his conscience, he took one more look up and down the road to check that it was clear and listened for the sound of any vehicles possibly approaching. He ran towards the lifeless body, now lying in a pool of red blood, a sickly copper stench emanating from the scene. It was all he could do to stop himself from throwing up.

He lifted the body. She felt cold, but he tried to put that down to the weather... even though it was a warm evening. 'Sorry,' he muttered under his breath. 'This wasn't meant to happen... Look, someone will find you and you'll be okay...' he whispered as he tried to avoid those eyes. They were like the eyes in paintings that follow you wherever you go.

As he pulled the hammer from beneath her, he knew she was dead. There was no doubt. He ran, sweating profusely, and threw the hammer in the same direction as he had thrown the gun. He felt relieved when a few thick drops of rain splashed against his head. The rain was getting heavier. It soaked through his clothes and the thoughts running through his mind shocked him; he was thinking that at least with the rain washing over him, the blood might wash out of his clothes... the evidence might disappear.

As he stood by the driver's door of his car and held onto the handle, he knew that he would not be able to get into the car until he had done one final thing. He had to get rid of the body. He would have to throw her over the edge of the cliff. If she landed on a rock it would seem like a suicide. People would think she'd jumped... *But what about the head wound? They'd think she hit her head on a rock whilst falling!* If she landed in the sea, she'd drift away and may never be found, he reasoned.

His thoughts frightened him—how he appeared to be taking this in his stride. *Maybe if I hadn't killed her, she would have taken the gun back and killed me? Yes... It was self-defence. She was a madwoman. She had wildness in her eyes. She was hardly an angel; she owned a handgun for God's sake. And she seemed confident. She wasn't innocent in all this.*

He tried to find a way to relieve himself of the guilt that was weighing him down; it was too heavy to carry. He kept repeating: *It was self-defence, I was only protecting myself... self-defence...*

Dragging her body to the cliff edge was a hard task, and in the pouring rain that soaked through his blood-splattered clothing, it felt even harder. He had heard that a body stiffens when a person dies; the heaviness of the body certainly did not seem normal. She was not a large woman, yet it took every ounce of energy left inside him to pull her off the road and onto the edge of the cliff. He stood panting as if he had run a marathon, aware that at any moment, a car could drive past. He would have to dispose of the body. In desperation, as quickly as possible, he lifted the dead girl as best he could and hurled her over the cliff edge, almost losing his footing and falling after her into the vast blackness that lay before him. For a few moments, he stood shaking at the fear of what could have been. Then, he realised again that he had somehow managed to put to the back of his mind the fact that he'd killed this woman, as if it were unimportant. Already, he was finding it difficult to live with the person he had become. It felt almost as though he had been taken over by another soul, coerced into doing what he had just done. After all, he, *Nigel Price*, wasn't capable of doing that. He was a hard-working man, a loving husband... He and June had even talked about starting a family. The man he had been before would have been shocked by what he had just done. This new version of him had a heart made of stone. But suddenly memories from the past, words of warning from friends and family, ambushed his conscience as he recalled that he had always had an aggressive streak: *'You'll meet your match one day, Nige... You be careful, Nige, the way you are behaving you'll get into real trouble one day... Calm down, Nige, it was only a joke, mate; you take everything so personally... Nige, you have to control your temper...'* He stood, holding his head, trying to rid it of the torrent of recalled snippets from the past... mainly from his teenage years and early twenties. *I've grown up since then; I'm not that boy, that angry boy...* But then the enormity of the situation presented itself again, and he couldn't deny reality. For years, he had fooled himself that he had let the anger of his youth dissipate; he'd believed that the bitterness and resentment that he'd felt towards his parents had been left in the past with his uncontrollable temper— uncontrollable because he had been so controlled by them. He had felt far more centered in his life since marrying June, and had thought he was a good man now. Here he was facing his demons once again.

He heard a loud scream and then realised it was his own. The rain continued showering him, but the blood stains remained on his clothes and hands, despite his frantic attempts to wash it away. One thing was for sure, the rain could not wash away the thoughts that were pervading his mind; could not wash away his sins. His tears began to fall again and mingled with the rain.

He walked back towards his car after taking a last desperate glance over the cliff and resisting the urge to follow the woman's lifeless body over the edge. That was the moment when the voice in his head began to torture him: *Murderer... murderer... murderer...* it chanted, and continued without stopping, never giving him a moment's peace.

I can't get into the car like this, there'll be blood everywhere... evidence. Nigel shivered. He racked his brain... *I need something to sit on.* He ran to the back of the car remembering that he had a few bin bags in there. He couldn't remember why they were in there, then his thoughts drifted for a moment... Could he have known that he was going to kill someone and would need these bags to line the seat of his car? He heard almost manic laughter in his head. It didn't sound like his own. *What's happening to me?* He concentrated hard trying to rid his mind of the echoes of that laughter.

Emily's car remained in his memory as he drove away from the scene. He had left her car right there in front of the traffic lights. There had been blood on the ground, next to it. As the rain battered against his windscreen, he prayed that the rain would fall hard enough and long enough to wash away the blood. He caught himself praying and wondered if God would even hear him now; now that he was a murderer. His mind went back to the pool of blood that had remained on the ground as he'd dragged the woman's body away towards the cliff... the trail of blood would show that she had been taken away from the scene. Forensics would surely work out that there had been foul play. He could not get the image of that bloodied body out of his mind. There was so much blood;

would the rain really be able to wash it away? Blood is thick... would it be possible? *There was so much of it.*

He could not rest; he had to return. *The criminal always returns to the scene of the crime...* the thought ran through his head, taunting him. He knew he had to move her car somewhere else, away from the scene; that would make it harder for the police to link the blood and the car.

He made a U-turn and drove back along the dark, treacherous road, now almost hoping that he could be the next fatality on this road; tempted to drive too fast or too close to the cliff edge. Another car approached. Panic surged through him. *Were there other cars passing while I was getting rid of the body? I didn't see any. But I wasn't looking for any. Oh my God, what if this is a police car? But, no, if it was the police, the sirens would be sounding... surely. There were those two... or three cars while I was arguing with her, but... were there more? Have they called the police?*

The car passed by without event, just another driver heading home after work. Nigel released the breath he hadn't even known he was holding. *How can I live like this? Constantly on edge. Maybe I should just hand myself in?*

His clothes were soaked through, his tears blurred his vision. He shifted uncomfortably on the plastic bin bag. He had tried his best to get the blood off his hands before touching the steering wheel, rubbing his hands together in the rain, trying to wash them, yet he could still feel that squelchy, stickiness on his palms, and he once more resisted the urge to throw up.

He soon arrived beside the pool of blood. It was still there, like a red river, seemingly growing larger rather than being diluted by the rain. Jumping out of his vehicle, he approached the victim's car. Shattered splinters of glass were covering the seats. He opened the boot to try to find something to sit on, and found a large holdall. It was empty. He decided to use the holdall as a seat cover.

The rain was still falling heavily. He sat in the driver's seat and after an initial panic was relieved to find that the dead girl had left her keys in the ignition. The car started after the second attempt.

The sweat was now pouring from his brow, mingling with the rain that was lashing down through the broken windscreen. His heart was beating fast. He was aware that at any moment another car could drive past. What would he look like driving away from a pool of blood in a car with smashed windows? He could only hope the darkness would obscure the suspicious circumstances. Again, he wrestled with his conscience; a girl was dead—probably at the bottom of the ocean by now—because of him, and here he was, no remorse, just wanting to get away and leave no trace. *Who am I? What have I become?* His tears now began to fall, joining in with the watery assault of rain and sweat.

As he started driving, he was unsure where he should leave the car. *It has to be far enough from the cliff edge to avoid the police looking for a body...* He remembered there was a lay-by about two hundred yards on the right, and an abandoned vehicle had been left there for months the year before. He'd always noticed it when he'd driven to and from work. He decided he would leave the car there. With any luck, this car would be ignored as well; people would just assume it had been dumped by its owner.

As he took the keys from the ignition and stepped out of the car, something caught his eye on the passenger seat; a handbag. The dead girl's handbag.

He leaned into the car and picked it up by the handle, hesitantly, using just his thumb and forefinger, as if it were a bomb about to explode. It was a small, red leather bag with a fabric rose design on one side. He knew he would have to dispose of it, but he didn't want to throw it over the cliff. If it was found, the police would then start looking for her body.

He didn't want to hold it for any longer than he had to. He unzipped it, looking inside as if for inspiration. Inside, there was a small purse, another set of keys, and a compact mirror and lipstick. Nothing else. Nothing that could identify the victim.

Victim. The word resounded in his mind. *Murderer... murderer... murderer...* He shook his head.

Hiding the bag under his jacket, and grabbing the holdall from the seat, he ran back towards his car. The road seemed never-ending. Rain pelted his face as he ran. By the time he reached his car, he was soaked through and shivering. He was out of breath and had to sit in the driver's seat for at least ten minutes before he could drive away.

When he got to the high street in his neighbourhood, he found the nearest public waste bin and threw the bag and holdall in there when no one was watching.

The rain continued to fall all night. Nigel lay awake, listening to the sound as it joined with his increased heartbeat and the repetitive chanting in his head; *murderer... murderer, murderer...* Needless to say, he did not sleep that night. His mind was in a whirl. What if the police found the car during the night? People might have reported it after he left; what then? And, someone may have been looking for that woman, she must have a family... she'd mentioned a boyfriend; he would wonder why she had not returned home. The police were probably scouring the town, looking for her; they might have found the body by now. He imagined hoards of police officers on that beach, helicopters, looking for someone... looking for him... it would only be a matter of time. They would handcuff him, ask him questions... lock him up and throw away the key. He tried to tell himself there was nothing to link him to the car. Anyone could have killed her. But all his mind would reply was, *You killed her.*

Then, he remembered the people who had driven past when he was arguing with the woman. Would they remember what he looked like? Sometimes people were very good at remembering features. There was something about how that young girl had looked at him; her face was sad. Had she noticed that there was a fight going on? Would she mention it to her parents? Would they hear it on the news and then go to the police? Maybe these witnesses would give an accurate description of him... and his car. They might have seen his car's number plate. The feeling of panic escalated.

He could not deny that it was possible someone would remember something that would identify him and put him there at the scene of the crime. It was dark and it had been raining, but with the lights from the cars, he could remember their faces. He would be able to pick them out from a lineup; he felt sure about that. So what about them? Surely, they, too, would remember him?

He could still picture the old man's face, the man who had appeared annoyed at having to overtake the dead woman's car on the narrow road. Nigel knew he'd be able to describe him to police. Perhaps that was what the old man was doing now—describing Nigel to the police.

Chapter 6

When weeks went by and there was no mention of the crime, the girl who'd gone missing, or even the car that had been abandoned, Nigel began to wonder at the life of someone who could just disappear and not be missed. He'd expected front page news at least in the local newspaper by now, and even a national news story about this mysterious girl's disappearance. He remembered watching a short film on TV once where a man had completely imagined meeting a girl and killing her... maybe that was what had happened here? It could all be in his mind. Perhaps she had never existed except as a figment of his imagination? That thought helped him to breathe easier for the first time in weeks, but then he realised that if that was the case, he would need to be concerned about the state of his mental health. His mind did not feel as though it belonged to him anymore; it contained endless chatter—chatter from voices he could not even recognise as his own, all with different theories about what had happened, if it had happened, and why it had happened. At nights he could not switch off. His eyes developed dark rings around them as a permanent feature; people were forever commenting that he looked tired or he looked unwell. How long before someone put two and two together and realised there was something wrong?

When people talked to him now, it was all he could do to stop himself from repeating what the voices in his head were saying; trying to keep them at bay meant that he hardly said a word. Surely his friends and family must think it odd. Not that he was ever a big conversationalist, but he'd had a loud voice in the past and he'd never been afraid to speak his mind or shout out if he didn't agree with what someone said to him. He had morphed into a person he didn't recognise: a silent, frightened, nervous man.

June had commented about it not long after the murder hit the news headlines, saying he didn't seem himself. They'd been getting dressed for bed.

'I'm worried about you, Nige. You seem miles away when I'm talking to you, and your eyes look haunted,' she said as she climbed into bed.

What is it with women's intuition anyway? *thought Nigel, angrily, but then he caught himself. He could not afford to be angry anymore; not since... He blanked out any further thought, never allowing his mind to wander into the realms of that night, afraid it might never return.*

'I'm fine,' he managed to say above his inner, deafening and taunting voices.

'Look, what's wrong?' she said, moving closer to him on the bed and looking into his eyes.

He turned away. 'It's just been stressful at work recently,' he said, almost under his breath.

'It's just like you to keep everything bottled up,' she said. 'Maybe we need a holiday. I was looking in some brochures at the local travel agent today. Spain would be nice. Shall I book us a holiday?'

Nigel had already thought about leaving the country, but for him, it was the idea of leaving the country for good that attracted him most. At the same time, he knew that even if he left the country he could not leave his guilt behind and all the voices in his head. He would just be running but never finding any peace. He pondered the idea of a holiday with June. Perhaps that would help in the short term, or would it just give him more time to think? More hours in the day of not doing anything. At least when he was at work he had the daily tasks to keep him occupied.

'Nige?' June was waiting for an answer.

'Um... let me think about it,' he said.

'Why haven't you been using your car to get to work?' she asked.

The car. *The image flashed in his mind. He had driven the car to work the day after the incident and was listening to the cassette he already had in there. As it had reached the end of side A, he had flipped it over when beginning his journey. On the way home, he'd been minding his own business, even singing along to some of the tracks, when the next song started playing...* How Will I Laugh Tomorrow... *He almost lost control of the car as his mind was taken back to the night before, the song reminding him of his carefree existence, when his conscience had been clear. One minute, he'd been happily singing along with the song, the next thing he knew, he was a murderer.*

As he slowed the car on the approach to a set of traffic lights that were still green, the driver of the car behind him sounded the horn in frustration. Nigel jumped at the loud beep and noticed his mistake. He drove through the lights, kicking himself for losing his concentration. I almost just did what she did... I almost caused an accident... That driver behind me could have gone straight into the back of my car. I almost stopped at a green light, instead of a red one. What's wrong with me? That driver was angry; he beeped his horn... But would he have killed me? He wouldn't have killed me. No one kills someone for making a mistake... he's not a murderer, like you, Nigel. Murderer... murderer... murderer...

He found a convenient place to park at the side of the road and took the cassette out of the car stereo, his hands shaking as he did so. He began to pull the tape out of the cassette—the slinky brown, shiny tape that reminded him of something he wanted to forget. He tried to tear it, but it was too hard, it just became thinner and longer. As he continued to pull it out of the cassette, he was left with just a curly, long length of brown, tangled string. The tears poured from his eyes, but he did not notice them or realise he was crying. He threw the cassette out of his passenger window onto the road and sped off home. The following day, he got into his car as usual to drive to work, but could not bring himself to put the key into the ignition; he felt something like fear. Since that day, he had taken the train to work while his car sat by the side of the road, a reminder of the worst night of his life. He wanted to have the car crushed in a scrap yard, but could not even bring himself to drive it to one. He thought about setting the car on fire and fantasised about watching it burn.

'I don't need the car anymore,' he replied to June.

'But... you used to love driving. What's happened to you, Nige? I hardly recognise you anymore. Even your voice has changed. It's like you're whispering sometimes. Maybe you need your ears tested. My uncle Ray used to suffer with excess ear wax, and he used to speak ever so quietly when his ears were blocked. It's something to do with not being able to hear the volume of your own voice; like deaf people. When he'd get his ears cleared out, his voice would go back to normal.'

If only wax was my problem. Nigel closed his eyes as if in silent prayer.

'And, when was the last time you had a shower?' continued June.

He sighed. 'I told you, it's been stressful at work. I'm thinking of selling the car,' he said quickly. He'd been thinking about it for weeks. The only thing that had stopped him was the fear that there might be some evidence in there. He'd been covered in blood and had sat at the steering wheel... There might be fibres... you always hear about police finding fibres from victims' clothing on the murderer. What if one of the woman's strands of hair got transferred from my clothes onto the car seat? What if some of her DNA could be found in my car? Her handbag was in there for a while.

'It's my car as well as yours, Nige,' said June, interrupting his train of thought. 'Just because I don't need it to travel to work doesn't mean I don't want to keep it. What about when the baby comes? We'll need the car then. And, it's handy for when we go shopping and visiting my friends and your parents. They live miles away.'

Nigel suddenly remembered his parents. Ever since the incident, he'd no space in his brain for anything but guilt, worry, *and concern. His parents were getting older, both in their seventies. He and June usually visited them at least once a month even though they lived about 60 miles away.*

'We really should go and see them soon,' said June. 'I spoke to your father last Wednesday. It was his birthday. They're overjoyed about the news of the pregnancy. Why didn't you tell them? I mentioned it to your father, and he didn't have a clue. He said you hadn't phoned him. Not even for his birthday. You usually do. He was worried about you. Remember I mentioned it to you when you got home from work?'

Nigel didn't remember that. He forgot many things these days, like the fact that he was supposed to have a shower, clean his teeth, eat, sleep, change his underwear. He'd been called to his manager's office at work twice since that fateful evening. Both times, he'd been warned that he had better "pull his socks up" or risk losing his job.

So they would have to keep the car. A reminder of that night. But then again, everything was a reminder of that night. Nigel could not relax. He felt like a wanted man; constantly on alert, waiting to be found out.

Chapter 7

By the time the news broke nationally about Emily Baxter's disappearance, Nigel was already in a deep state of depression. The regret for what he had done ate away at him slowly. It lived with him, side by side.

Emily Baxter had been driving a stolen car the night he'd killed her. When Nigel first heard this, he felt almost relieved. Perhaps she had been a criminal, had committed a crime and was making a getaway in a stolen car. Perhaps she'd even killed someone. If that was the case, surely Nigel would not be so severely punished if he was ever found out. Killing a murderer was not as bad as killing an innocent girl, was it? Or was it all one and the same: murder. Besides, he hadn't known she was a criminal when he killed her, hadn't been taking revenge for a crime she'd committed. He'd just killed her, plain and simple, without knowing who she was.

Nigel had only overheard a snippet of the news as he walked past the living room: 'Emily Baxter disappeared in August this year. She had been driving a stolen vehicle. It was abandoned...'

That was all he'd heard. He hadn't stopped; didn't want to hear any more. Maybe it was because that short burst of information made him feel better and hearing anything more might just ruin it. But he felt curious afterwards and wished he had listened further. He might have found out that she was a serial killer who had been on the police wanted lists for years and he had been the hero who'd killed her—her just punishment for taking innocent lives.

It wasn't long before June brought it up in a conversation that evening.

'That girl, Emily Baxter, she'd been driving a stolen car when she went missing. It was her boyfriend's, apparently; he bought it from a man in a pub, or so he says. Told police he didn't know the name of the man who sold it to him. It's all a bit suspicious, if you ask me; I mean, people need to have a log book when they buy a car, and they need to fill in a form when it's transferred to someone else. You'd think Emily's boyfriend would have asked questions, wouldn't you?'

Nigel hated the way June talked about Emily Baxter, using her first name as if she'd known her. It felt odd, familiarising her, making her seem like a person they would have been friends with; that June would have been friends with.

'Anyway, when the police found the car,' continued June, not waiting for Nigel to reply—having become used to his silence, probably, as he hardly spoke anymore; 'they didn't link it to Emily's disappearance because they thought it had been dumped by the criminals who stole it; joyriders, maybe. When the car was found, her parents hadn't even reported her missing yet. Emily wasn't known to the police. I think Russ is the one who killed her.'

Nigel hadn't heard much of what June had said after, "Emily wasn't known to the police". That was enough to cause him to sink back into depression. The brief shaft of light that had made him think he might still have a chance at redemption was obliterated. Emily was an innocent woman; she wasn't a criminal... and he had killed her.

***

Nigel had somehow managed to get through the working week where the most talked-about subject in the office was Emily Baxter's murder. On Saturday, June had gone out with one of her friends and left him alone in the house. He had stayed in bed until noon, and then began to think about getting up. Sleep wasn't the same for Nigel since he had killed Emily. It was something that eluded him. No matter how tired he was, he would not be able to sleep. He would lie for hours until he could no longer bear the sound of his conscience, then take a sleeping pill to try to drown everything out. Many a night, he had contemplated taking a few sleeping pills just to end it all, but somehow, he never went ahead with the plan.

He got out of bed and walked into the bathroom. Catching sight of his appearance in the mirror, he frowned. He could no longer bear to look at his own face. He could not make eye contact with his reflection; it was like he was facing a stranger, someone he despised, someone who had ruined his life.

He pulled off his pyjamas, about to step into the shower when the doorbell rang. Nigel wanted to ignore it, but what if it was someone for June? She had been having a go at him recently about how he never answered the phone or the door and always expected her to do it. He knew she was waiting for a parcel to be delivered; she had left a note on the bedside table letting him know. She would only nag him even more if he didn't answer the door.

As he pulled on his dressing gown and made his way down the stairs, a familiar fantasy played in his head. He would open the door now and there would be two police officers standing there, ready to arrest him for the murder of Emily Baxter. He would hold out his hands and accept the handcuffs, breathing a sigh of relief at not having to hide anymore. He braced himself as he opened the door, and was relieved to see it wasn't policemen. At the same time, he hated himself for being such a coward.

Distracted by his thoughts, Nigel didn't greet the visitor at the door. He merely stood and stared straight ahead. The man at the door was his neighbour, from two doors down. Pete Wilkinson. Before the events of the 19th of August 1991, Nigel and Pete had been quite good friends. They sometimes even went to the local pub together at the weekend, and often stood for an hour or so chatting outside their doors when they bumped into each other at the weekends or after work. But since the murder, Nigel had avoided Pete. He would only say "hello" if he saw him in the street and make up some excuse about being busy, or in a hurry to be somewhere.

'All right, Nige?' said Pete, snapping Nigel out of his reverie.

'Hi, Pete. Um... I was just about to jump into the shower,' he said.

'I won't keep you. I just wanted to borrow a hammer. Luce is insisting that I fix a shelf that has been falling down since August, and I finally had enough of the nagging today, but can't find my hammer. I'm sure I lent it to you at some stage. Do you still have it?'

Nigel's face turned white. The hammer he had killed Emily with belonged to Pete. He had borrowed it from him back in January and never returned it. They were such good friends, he'd not felt that he had to rush to return it.

'Nige?' Pete's eyes widened. 'You look a bit pale, mate. Are you feeling okay?'

'Um... I didn't sleep well.'

'Okay, well, look, I'll leave you in peace. Luce has been waiting for months for the shelves to be fixed, a few more days won't hurt. When you find the hammer, bring it round, okay?'

'Okay,' said Nigel.

'And, when you're feeling better, let's go out for a few pints. I've missed our chats. Those two guys we used to wind up in the pub, Evan and Jake, have been asking where you are!'

Nigel nodded and closed the door without replying.

Why was Pete asking for the hammer back now? Nigel felt a paranoia creep through his mind. Did he know something? Okay, so Nigel had been avoiding him, but he hadn't really made an effort for them to get together since August. Why did he ask for the hammer now? The news report about Emily's death said something about the forensics team thinking she was hit on the head with a blunt instrument. "It might have been a hammer" were the words used.

Nigel's mind felt cloudy as he thought back to the night he had returned home after disposing of Emily's body. He remembered now that Pete had waved at him from his door when He had gone outside to dump his shredded and bloodied clothes into the bin. Pete always stood outside his front door when he was smoking a cigarette as his wife never let him smoke in the house. Nigel had waved back at him that night, but then he had run inside the house and closed the door quickly, not wanting a conversation with Pete... with anyone, for that matter.

Did Pete suspect something? Had he seen the news report about Emily's death and remembered that he'd seen Nigel late at night on that date? The porch light had been on. What if Nigel had some blood on his face? Would Pete have been able to notice it from that distance, two doors down?

The thoughts whizzed furiously around Nigel's brain, and although the rational part of him knew that there was no way Pete could have known he had anything to do with Emily's murder, he couldn't relax. What if Pete had read about the forensic investigators saying she was most likely killed by a hammer blow? What if he wanted to see if Nigel still had the hammer because he suspected that Nigel had something to do with it?

Nigel could not stop the negative, irrational thoughts swimming around in his brain until he felt quite nauseated.

Later that day, he went out and bought a new hammer for Pete, trying to find one that looked the same. As he stood in the queue at the hardware shop waiting to pay for it, sweat was dripping from his brow, he felt physically sick, and a panic took hold of him, making him want to run. He arrived home with the hammer and began to cry openly as he sat on the sofa in the lounge.

June walked into the room and saw him; he was still wearing his coat and boots, the bag from the hardware shop on the coffee table in front of him.

'N... N... Nige? What happened?'

He quickly wiped his tears with his sleeve and grabbed a bunch of tissues from the box on the table. 'I didn't know you were home!' he said, aggressively, angrily, as he pushed past her. Then he rushed back into the living room to pick up the plastic bag containing the hammer. He felt mortified that June had caught him crying. She would ask so many questions now. His conscience was also questioning his mood. Why was he allowing himself to get so angry, so out of control? Fear caused a rush of adrenaline to race through his veins. His heart beat faster. *You can't get angry, Nigel, can't allow it. If you do, you might kill June... You're a murderer...murderer... murderer...*

'Is everything all right?' she shouted after him, worry colouring her voice.

'Yes!' he boomed, as he ran upstairs and slammed the bedroom door behind him, fighting to keep a grip on the last vestiges of his sanity.

Half an hour later, he had calmed down sufficiently to be able to take the hammer to Pete's house. Lucy, Pete's wife, opened the door. 'Hi, Nigel, it's been a long time! Come in.'

'No, no,' he said softly. 'I'm just bringing back Pete's hammer. Well, actually it's a new one. The one I borrowed from him broke.' Nigel had toyed with the idea of trying to make the hammer look old, but the one Pete had lent him was so worn, rusting in parts with stains of paint on the handle... he would never be able to get it to look the same.

'Pete!' shouted Lucy.

Pete came running along the hallway.

'Hi, Nige! Come in, mate.'

'No, I don't have time. I was just returning your hammer,' he said, handing him the orange plastic bag.

'My what? Sorry, I couldn't hear you very well.'

'Er... your hammer,' said Nigel, trying to raise his voice a notch.

'Ah, okay, thanks.'

'It's a new one because yours broke.'

'Oh, Nige, don't worry, mine was old. Here, you keep this one,' he said, holding out the plastic bag towards him.

'No, no, it's okay. I want you to have it,' replied Nigel, taking a step back as if there was a bomb in the bag.

'That's really good of you, mate. Sure you won't come in for a pint?'

'No, sorry,' said Nigel, looking at the ground.
'Okay, well, some other time then,' said Pete.
Nigel nodded and walked away.

Chapter 8

On the evening of the 19th of August 1991, Emily had left home after a heated argument with her boyfriend. She'd left home in the clothes she was wearing, not bothering to take anything with her, just her shoulder bag. Over the weeks, she had been taking her belongings bit by bit to her lover's house. She had planned to leave Russell, her boyfriend of thirteen years, for Ramiro, her new man.

That night, Emily had deliberately started an argument with Russell, knowing she would have to leave him *now*. She was three months pregnant. Time was running out and soon it would be obvious for all to see. It was Ramiro's child she was carrying. She didn't love Russell anymore; she'd fallen out of love with him when she'd found out he was involved with a local gang that had been responsible for many crimes in the area.

She had seen a different side to Russell. He had fooled her, making her think he was hard working, but the truth was for the past three years or so, he'd been mixed up with a gang he had drifted into when he lost his job. Since then, although he said he was working, she'd discovered he'd been working part-time jobs as a cover-up but also helping out the gang with its own "jobs". The first she knew of his criminal activities was about a year before her death, when their neighbour, Mr. Jackson, an elderly man who suffered from Parkinson's disease, came to see Emily and Russell before he left for a hospital appointment and asked if they would keep an eye on his dog. He gave them his keys.

When the old man had left, Russell told her that he was going out to get a newspaper. Later that day, their neighbour came to collect his keys and invited them over for a cup of tea to thank them for looking after the dog. Russell said he couldn't because he'd already agreed to meet a friend to discuss a possible job opportunity. Emily felt sorry for Mr. Jackson, so she went to his house for tea.

Emily helped the old man make the tea because his right hand was shaky due the Parkinson's. He told her he was always afraid he would scald himself. 'I do have a carer who comes over a couple of times a day, but she's not always around when I want a cup of tea,' he said, laughing. He was in quite good spirits.

Emily smiled. Whisky, his pet Labrador, followed him and nuzzled against his legs, appearing happy to have him home.

'I've been thinking of selling this place and getting a bungalow or a ground-floor flat. Somewhere smaller. It gets a bit much for me, the cleaning. It's much too big for me, this place. It was okay when my wife was alive and when our children lived here. Now they've gone. My Cindy lives in America now, and Jason lives in Canada. They send me birthday cards, Christmas cards, Father's Day. They're always going on at me to visit them, but I'm not in good health, and those countries seem so far away. They've got small children and busy lives, so they can't visit me. I do talk to them on the phone, but it gets expensive.' He had a sad look on his face as she picked up the cups of tea and placed them on the kitchen table.

He sat down across from her. Then as she looked up at him, she saw his eyes widen and his mouth fall open. 'Oh!' he exclaimed, standing up shakily.

'Are you okay?' asked Emily. She also stood up, worried about him, in fear that he might be having a heart attack or something.

'Um... I'm not sure, dear. I... my... the microwave is missing. He turned around. 'And the silver carriage clock I had on the table.'

Then, he looked at her and placed his hand—which was shaking quite violently—over his mouth. He pointed at her with his other hand and shook his head. She saw tears form in his eyes as he lowered his hand from his mouth. 'I... I gave you my keys when I went out. It was you, wasn't it? What else have you taken?'

'No, Mr. Jackson. I promise you.'

'But I asked you to keep an eye on the dog. You had my keys.'

Whisky sat next to his master, whimpering as if he could feel his pain.

Emily wondered whether this was some kind of setup. Was he going to try to get some money from them? 'How dare you blame me?' she said, offended. 'I didn't take your things. I wouldn't do that!'

'Then who did?' he asked. His face looked so sad, she didn't have the heart to raise her voice to him again. He couldn't be lying. He couldn't be that good an actor.

'Mr. Jackson, I'm sorry if you've been burgled, but it wasn't me, okay? Look, I'll help you call the police.'

So she spent the rest of the day with Mr. Jackson and two police officers who came to look around his house and assess what had been taken. They took a statement from him.

The old man was clearly traumatised by the event. He did a lot of crying. Emily's tears also welled up a few times.

When she returned home later that evening, she saw lots of bric-a-brac on the coffee table in the front room: watches, glasses, ornaments, jewellery, coins. Russ was singing to himself in the kitchen.

She made her way into the kitchen. The first thing she noticed was a microwave oven. They didn't own a microwave oven. 'Where did you get that from?'

'My friend, Rob, was helping a mate with a house clearance and got a lot of stuff. I went over earlier, and he said I could take some. This is good,' he said, pointing at the microwave oven. 'It's a quality brand. Quite new, as well. There's some jewellery in there on the coffee table I thought you might like.'

'You stole this from Mr. Jackson, didn't you?' As Emily said the words, it was almost as though she was unable to comprehend them. *How could this have happened?*

Russell looked at her, his mouth open, then he seemed to find his bearings. He shrugged. 'So what?'

'Take it back!" screamed Emily, at the top of her voice. Her nerves were fraught from spending the day with a man who had lost bits of his life, and Russell was behaving as if it didn't mean anything.

Russell looked at her, his face telling her he thought she had lost her mind. 'Fuck off, Ems. I'm not taking this stuff back. He's probably reported it to the pigs by now. I'll get nicked. Anyway, I don't feel sorry for him. He can claim on his insurance.'

'Take it when he's not in. Just return it!' she screamed.

'No!' shouted Russell. Then he walked towards her and put his face very close to hers. 'Let's get one thing straight here: you don't tell me what to do, okay?'

'This isn't you, Russ!' she said, moving away, slightly intimidated by a look in his eyes she didn't recognise. He'd never looked at her like that before. There was a deep and dark void that used to be his pupils, as if he could swallow her up with just one stare.

He twisted around and walked back to the microwave. It had just beeped to let him know his food was ready. 'Get used to it, bitch. This is the new improved Russell Banks.' He turned and winked at her, a wide grin on his face. 'Before you know it, we'll be millionaires. Stick with me, baby.' He laughed and breezed past her into the living room with a bowl of soup.

Emily was left speechless. She followed him into the room and watched as he slurped his soup noisily while looking at the items on the table.

'What are you going to do with all this stuff?' she said, trying to avoid making him angry again. He was in an unpredictable mood.

'I'm gonna sell it, baby. Me and you are gonna be rich!'

'But it's just an old man's stuff. It's got sentimental value to him... It's not worth anything.'

'I've got a friend who can sell it for me. He can get a good price.'

Emily shook her head, her eyes drawn to the items on the table. She noticed a ring and remembered Mr. Jackson saying that his wife's ruby ring had been taken. He'd been in floods of tears as he'd explained how she'd worn it every day since they got engaged, and had been wearing it when she died. He said he could always feel her presence, as if she was right there in the room with him, when he picked it up. In fact, he hadn't stopped talking about the ring for much of the afternoon.

Emily walked towards the table and picked up the ring.

'Hey, don't touch what you can't afford,' said Russell, laughing.

She put on the sweetest smile she could muster. 'But Russ, didn't you say I could have the jewellery? You said you got it for me.'

He narrowed his eyes, then shrugged. 'Okay. Look, you can have that ring if you like it so much, but we have to sell the other stuff or we won't make much money.'

'Thanks,' she said, smiling again.

She put the ring on her finger.

'Suits your hair, Ems,' said Russell. He finished his soup and stood up. 'Right, I've got to go and get rid of this lot now. I'll see you later.'

She felt helpless as he packed Mr. Jackson's belongings into a large box and took them to his car.

He returned and took the microwave. 'Sorry, hun, we can't keep this.'

She watched him drive away and hated him completely at that moment.

When the car had disappeared, she left the flat and knocked on Mr Jackson's door. He came to the door after a few minutes. His eyes were wet with fresh tears, and her heart went out to him.

'Hi, Mr. Jackson.'

'Emily. Thank you for helping me today, dear.'

'That's okay. Um... I found this on the pavement. I think the burglar must have dropped it. Is it one of the items that was stolen?' She reached out and handed him the ring.

His face brightened, and a smile slowly crept across it. 'Oh, this is wonderful. It's my Hilda's ring. I know this is a sign from her, to tell me that she's still with me.' He looked into her eyes. 'You're a good girl, Emily. Thank you for returning this. It is so dear to me. Some things can be replaced, but this is so special. God bless you for caring.' He reached out and touched her hand. She clasped his hand in both of hers.

'I just wish I could have brought the other things, too,' she said, her throat catching on the words, tears in her eyes.

'You're a good girl, Emily,' he repeated, then nodded and closed the door.

She returned to the flat next door and cried until she thought she would run out of tears.

Although Russell had been part of a gang for many years, Emily only found out a few weeks after Mr. Jackson had been burgled, when a package was delivered to their door by a burly man who insisted on seeing Russell.

When she'd asked Russell what was in the package, he'd said it was for his work. He worked in town as a delivery man for a pizza restaurant, so she was suspicious about that. He said it was a box containing new flyers that he had to hand out to customers, but when she asked to see them, he refused to show her.

Later, she caught him looking in the box, which he'd hidden under their bed. There were packets containing white powder; drugs. Slowly she pieced things together. *He must be taking those drugs...* It would explain his changing moods and the way he sometimes scared her with just one look. She walked into the room and confronted him. He had that terrifying look again now, and she had to turn away from his angry stare.

He pushed the box further under the bed and stood up slowly. 'You haven't seen anything,' he said. 'Do you hear me?' He almost whispered the words.

'But—' she began.

He grabbed her arm and pushed her against the door, shocking her, as he had not once been violent towards her in the past. She looked into his eyes and saw the pinprick pupils... wasn't that a sign of someone who'd been taking drugs? Or did the pupils dilate more? Fear surged through her.

He placed a hand on her neck. She struggled to breathe as he warned, 'You tell anyone about this, you're dead.'

Over the next few days, she came to learn the name of the gang he was involved in—The East Side Tigers, they called themselves, as if they were some kind of football or rugby team. She felt sick to her stomach.

After finding all this out, Emily could hardly bear to look at Russell.

Ramiro was a colleague at work. She was an administrator at the local council offices, and he worked in the same department. They had a lot in common. They liked the same music, books, TV programmes. Over the four years they had worked together, they'd become good friends. As she fell out of love with Russell, she began to fall in love with Ramiro, who had recently divorced his wife of eight years. Emily had been his shoulder to cry on, and soon became a lot more.

In July, she'd discovered she was pregnant and knew it was Ramiro's child; she hadn't slept with Russell since he'd burgled Mr. Jackson's house; they'd been living separate lives.

Chapter 9

August 19th 1991

Emily Baxter walked out of the flat she shared with Russell and slammed the door behind her. She had taken the keys to his car, when he'd been in the toilet, then she'd started the argument that had led to her leaving the flat. A sense of freedom washed over her. No longer would she have to endure the claustrophobic atmosphere of living in a house with someone who treated her with little respect. Ever since she'd found out he was associated with crime, a wall had been built brick by brick between them; a wall made up of cold stares, caustic words, and embarrassing silences. She could not live like that.

Tonight, she had brought up the burglary again as an excuse—a way to wind herself up and make it easier for her to let out all the anger she held towards him.

'You've never apologised for stealing Mr. Jackson's things!' she said, after he'd taken another suspicious box into their bedroom when he returned from work. She'd grabbed his keys off the sideboard where he'd dropped them when he came in, and waited for him to come out of the toilet.

'What are you talking about?' he said, frowning.

'Do you know where your gang took Mr. Jackson's things?'

'Er... I sold them. You know that. Anyway, you took that ruby ring, so don't act all innocent.'

'I took it so I could give it back to him.'

'What?'

'You're disgusting! How could you steal from an old man who is all alone and ill?'

'Look, it's no big deal; he has insurance. And I bet he's alone and ill because he's a fucking loser. His kids probably left the country to get away from him.' Russell laughed.

'Mr. Jackson is a nice old man, and his kids went abroad for work and decided to stay because they liked it there. They keep in touch with him.'

'No one ever ends up alone if they're a decent person,' said Russell, shaking his head. 'That weirdo next door deserves all he's got.'

'Oh shut up, Russ.'

'No, you shut up, you fucking bitch! The reason he's ill as well is because he's all fucking twisted inside and his body is just reflecting that.' His eyes were wild as he stared into hers. 'You need to wise up,' he said, pointing a finger at his head as if to indicate she was crazy. 'Stop feeling sorry for fucking creeps.'

Emily backed away from him to avoid the stale odour of his breath.

'You should be treating me with more respect,' he continued. 'If you carry on like this, I'll fucking throw you out and you can go and live with fucking Mr. Jackson for all I care, and find out for yourself why no one wants to fucking live with him.'

'You don't know anything about Mr. Jackson. When was the last time you bothered to stop and talk to him?'

'Oh, fuck off, Ems. Why would I wanna talk to a geriatric? Are you going soft in the head?'

'Mr. Jackson is a good man. He's alone and ill, not through any fault of his own, and you stole his stuff. You're the worst kind of person, Russ. You've changed so much, I don't recognise you anymore. I used to love you, but now I can't even bear to be in the same room as you,' said Emily, loudly, feeling as if a weight was being lifted from her.

'Really? I couldn't tell. Is that why you haven't been sleeping in the same bed as me for the past few months?' he said sarcastically. 'I don't know why you're being so self-righteous about it. If you really care that much about Mr. Jackson, how come you never visit him? You're a hypocrite. I remember you once complaining that he always lets the dog poo in the garden.'

A shot of guilt shook Emily. Could it be that Russell had burgled Mr. Jackson's house because of something she'd said about him? Maybe she'd been letting off steam absent-mindedly one day and he'd taken it to mean that she didn't like Mr. Jackson. In his warped mind, he could have used that as an excuse to take revenge on her behalf.

'Mr. Jackson is a nice old man, and I visit him when I can,' she said, as if trying too late to make up for anything that could endanger the old man's life.

'You realise that I'm sleeping with someone else,' he said, quite suddenly and unexpectedly.

She lowered her eyes and wondered who the poor unfortunate girl could be. Probably a tragic lost soul who had got in with the wrong crowd and was now so addicted to drugs she had to have sex with Russ so he could supply her with her next hit. Emily sometimes wondered what had possessed her to find Russ attractive. Looking at him in recent weeks she often felt repulsed; his hair was always greasy and lank and he had developed a spotty complexion and had lost a lot of weight. He'd always been of slim build anyway, but now he appeared emaciated.

'Don't look surprised,' he said.

I'm surprised anyone would sleep with you, she thought as she raised her eyes to look at him.

'I'm a man. I have needs. If you're not going to satisfy them, there are plenty of women ready and willing.' He walked towards her, his eyes seemingly unable to focus. His left eyebrow twitched, as it often did recently—a facial tic he appeared to have developed due to the drug abuse. His hand shook as he pointed at her.

79

He walked up to her and placed a hand on her cheek. 'Don't worry, you are still my number one girl; you say the word and I'll get rid of Angel. She's only a substitute.' He wore a half crazed smile on his face, bringing forth memories of Jack Nicholson in *One Flew Over The Cuckoo's Nest.*

She pulled away from him. 'If you think I'd ever let your filthy hands near me again, you're mistaken.' That was the excuse she needed to walk out of the door.

Emily got into Russell's car. He had brought the car home the week before, saying he'd won it in a poker game. She never asked questions about anything he brought home anymore; they were always things that had fallen off the backs of lorries or won in card games. Drug money was most likely the root of where everything really came from, but she'd stopped caring. She had disassociated herself from Russell in her heart and mind.

She drove to the end of the road and phoned her mother from a pay phone.

'I've left Russ. Don't ask why. Things just didn't work out.'

'Oh,' came the response. There was silence on the line for a moment, then her mother asked: 'Where are you going to stay?'

'I've got a friend. I'm not going to be in touch for a while, Mum, but don't worry about me. I'll be fine. Russ will be looking for me, he'll be angry and he associates with criminals, so I don't want you to know where I am, or he'll try to force it out of you. It's best if I just disappear for a while.'

'No, Emily—'

'Please don't try to talk me out of it. I've made up my mind. Give it a couple of months to blow over and I'll be in touch. I can't risk visiting you because I have another man, and I'm... Well, Russ might get jealous. You know what he's like.'

'But Emily, don't just disappear. I hate it when you row with Russell and go off for weeks without letting us know where you are. Do you have any idea how much I worry about you?'

'I'll be fine, Mum. I'll be with Ramiro, he's my new man. Oh, and I've given up my job, gave them my notice last month. I can't risk Russell turning up there. I have it all worked out. I've been planning it for months. Russ is into all sorts of criminal activity; I don't want anything more to do with him.'

'Why can't you just come home and stay with me and your father, Emily? You'll be safe here.'

'No, I wouldn't. I'm better off staying with Ramiro.'

'How do I know this Ramiro is not as bad as Russell? We've never met him.'

'He's a good man, Mum. I love him.'

'You loved Russell once.'

'Russ is bad news. Look, he might not try to find me, anyway. We had a row and I found out he's seeing someone else, so with any luck, he'll be her problem now. We've been living separate lives for the past few months. I just want to play it safe for a while, though. I know he can be hot-headed, and if he finds out about Ramiro he might try to cause trouble. As soon as I know he isn't looking for me anymore, I'll be in touch.'

'Keep in touch by phone, dear, and let me know how you are. There's no reason you can't do that.'

'I can't phone you, Mum. I don't want to put you in any danger or in an awkward position. This way, if Russ asks you about me you can just say you don't know where I am and you haven't heard from me, without having to lie.'

'You can be so stubborn at times, Emily.'

'Just know I'll be okay with Ramiro; he's a great guy. I can't wait for you to meet him. When we're settled and I'm sure Russ won't cause trouble, I'll be in touch. I have to go, Mum, my money is running out. Love you.'

Emily thought of the baby as she stepped out of the phone booth. She touched her stomach. Her parents would be so happy to have a grandchild. A smile played on her lips.

Chapter 10

Ramiro had waited for Emily the night before, but she hadn't arrived. He'd spent a sleepless night worrying about her. He had no way of getting in contact with her. He couldn't phone her home number in case Russell picked it up, and she had quit her job, so how would he be able to find her? Why hadn't she called him? It was easy enough to find a phone box even if she couldn't call him from home. Why would she let him worry like this? Paranoia taunted him; what if Emily didn't really love him? They had communicated every day at work, and had spent more and more time together outside of work. Now suddenly he felt adrift. She was no longer there. This dream had shattered so quickly. He couldn't help feeling naïve. *What was I thinking, getting involved with someone who was living with another man?* But his ego would not let him believe that it had all been lies. Emily had told him she loved him. She had told him that she'd been planning to leave Russell. *What if she's changed her mind?* He cursed his luck with women, and wished he'd never laid eyes on her. But then, another thought took precedence: what if she had told Russell she was leaving him and he had become angry?

He remembered her saying that she'd found out Russell was a drug addict. *Has he hurt her? Threatened her? Is that why she isn't here?* A disturbing image filled Ramiro's mind: Emily lying dead. Was Russell capable of murder? Maybe he had killed her in a fit of rage, finding out she was going to leave him for her lover.

Ramiro tossed and turned all night. He'd got out of bed a few times and wandered around the flat, finding a few of Emily's belongings wherever he went. She had been so sure she wanted to leave Russell. She'd brought most of her stuff here. But as he pondered this, he came to realise that most of the stuff she had brought here was replaceable: clothes, bric-a-brac, books. There was nothing that could be called *essential,* that she wouldn't be able to live without.

As he ate his breakfast the next morning, he became more and more frustrated. The lack of sleep made him edgy. He was supposed to be going to work, but he could not concentrate. He phoned in sick and then got into his car to try to find out what could have happened.

His first stop was Emily's flat—the one she shared with Russell. He'd never been there before, and his anxiety heightened as he reached the turning into the street. He could see the house at the end of the road. He knew that Emily and Russell had shared the first-floor flat for over 13 years. Jealousy caused his heart to skip a few beats, but he took a deep breath to calm himself. *She loves me, not Russell,* he thought, trying to convince himself. What if she was in there with Russell right now? What if, when she had told him that she was leaving, they had managed to iron out their differences? Emily was a trusting girl. Russell might have promised to leave the gang for her. Ramiro remembered her saying that when she'd first met Russell, he was a decent man. She believed he'd been led astray by his friends. Maybe he was so shocked that she was leaving him that he knew he had to change in order to keep her. Ramiro knew how it felt to be in love with Emily. She was so precious to him, he would do anything to keep her, never let her go. Perhaps Russell felt the same. Perhaps he'd told her lies to keep her with him.

Ramiro shook his head, trying to evict the unwelcome thoughts. It would have to be a fight to the death like in those old movies when there were two men in love with the same woman and they would fight, sword in hand, for the love of their life. Ramiro gripped the steering wheel hard as if preparing himself for battle.

He parked his car a few doors down from the house and sat waiting, even though he was not sure what he was waiting for. Would Emily even be in there? Then the thought occurred to him that if she'd decided not to leave Russell, she would probably not be leaving her job either. He would have to see her at work every day and know that he could never be with her. That would be difficult.

Ramiro thought about how vital Emily's support had been during his acrimonious divorce. He doubted he would have made it through without her.

Darcia, his ex-wife, had packed all his things and left them in suitcases outside their house one day, completely out of the blue. She'd sent him to the local supermarket that morning, a Sunday, with a long list of grocery items she wanted him to purchase.

Upon returning from the supermarket, Ramiro had tried to get into the house but found that the locks had been changed. He'd knocked on the door countless times and sat outside in the rain all day, listening to the sounds of his two children playing indoors. Darcia had shouted at him through the letterbox a few times, telling him he was not welcome there anymore and he should leave or she would call the police. She never did call the police.

His eldest, Isabella, had spoken to him through the letterbox.

'Why are you outside, Daddy? It's raining. You should come in.' She was four years old.

Eventually Darcia had rounded up the children and taken them upstairs. He heard her say, 'Daddy won't be living here anymore. He has to go away.'

Ramiro had racked his brain that evening and all through the night, not knowing why he had been thrown out. He had done nothing wrong. There was no reason why, as far as he could discern, that she should have chosen that particular day to throw him out. They'd had their ups and downs like any other couple, but he had not seen this coming.

The next morning, he had woken up in a puddle of water outside the house. His neck and back were stiff. Standing up had been almost impossible. His clothes were wet through, and he had developed a chill. It was 6.30 a.m. He thought about waiting there until Darcia left the house to take the children to nursery. But he was shivering from the cold that emanated from inside his body, so his first concern was to somehow get a change of clothes and wrap up warm. Besides, he couldn't let the children see him like that.

He picked himself up and took the two suitcases that Darcia had packed for him. He decided he would clean himself up somehow and then try to get in touch with her to talk things through.

His mind was spinning. What had he done? He didn't have a clue. He began to become paranoid, as he wondered whether he had done something without realising it; whether he had lost his mind temporarily and completely forgotten what he'd done. He took some of the grocery items with him, those that had not been completely ruined by the rain.

Darcia and Ramiro had been married for over eight years and had two children, Isabella and Damon. Isabella was the eldest. Damon was two and a half.

Darcia had seemed like the ideal partner when he'd met her over twelve years before. She was quiet and kept herself to herself. He'd met her at a friend's wedding and had been told that she'd recently come out of a difficult long-term relationship. She did have a sad, dejected look about her, but strangely that was one of the things that attracted him. He had been in a long-term relationship of over six years with a beautiful girl called Matilda, and he had thought she was the love of his life, but she'd had an affair. Although she tried to apologise and said it was only a one night stand and only happened because he was neglecting her, he had not been able to face up to any shortcomings he might have. They'd split up, and he'd gone through the worst two years of his life after that, trying to come to terms with it. Part of him wished he had given Matilda another chance, but the other part of him would not accept her betrayal.

So when he met Darcia for the first time and saw that battered look, he fell for her, thinking he'd found a kindred spirit. This woman had been hurt before by someone she loved. He vowed to make it all better.

Things went well for the first couple of years, while they were dating. They spent a lot of time together and Darcia always pandered to his every desire. The one thing that nagged him was how she seemed reluctant to spend time with his family. This meant that he was seeing his parents and his siblings less and less. They had always been close, but now that part of his life was having to be shelved to avoid upsetting Darcia. It was a small price to pay, he reasoned, if he could find happiness. He felt that he had wasted a lot of time in the wrong relationships, and now he really wanted to settle down and have children before it was too late. He was getting older, and many of his peers were already settled with families.

It was only natural, wasn't it, for a woman to want to spend time only with her partner without the interruption of extended family? Or so he thought.

After Ramiro married Darcia, things changed quite dramatically in his family life. She changed. It was as if now that they were married, she felt she could order him about and set all the rules in their relationship. It was almost an overnight transformation.

As time went by, the relationship between Ramiro and his parents suffered. Darcia did not want to visit his family. She kept repeating to him that they would soon make a family of their own.

Ramiro's brother and sister told him that they found Darcia distant, and they raised a concern that he seemed to be drifting away from them. He tried to explain that Darcia was a private person, a timid woman. All the while, however, there had been a nagging doubt in his head. Something wasn't quite right. But Darcia was his chance to make something of himself after years of failed relationships. He would not give in. He would try to make everything better.

When Isabella was born, Ramiro was happy to be a father. It was a dream come true, and he began to put Darcia on a pedestal.

She was the mother of his child and could do no wrong. But rather than bringing him and Darcia closer to his own family, the gap was widened by the birth of his child. Naturally, his parents and siblings wanted to be a part of Isabella's life, but Darcia behaved in a way that came across as selfish to Ramiro's family; she was very controlling over the welfare of the child. She made it clear on a few occasions that she did not want the outside influence of his parents or his brother and sister. This caused arguments and bitter disputes until eventually Ramiro and Darcia cut their ties with the rest of his family.

Ramiro began to realise that Darcia's relationship with her own family was distant, and he questioned himself as to how and why he hadn't noticed that before. It became a strain on Ramiro, realising that he had let his family down. He missed them and felt bad that they could not see how Isabella was growing up to be so bright and beautiful. The child reminded him so much of his mother. A tear would come to his eye when he looked into her brown eyes and saw the resemblance. But he did not have time to rectify the situation because Darcia announced she was pregnant again when Isabella was just over a year old.

Needless to say, by the time Darcia had given birth to Damon, Ramiro had lost all contact with his own family. They didn't phone or visit anymore, and Darcia always had an excuse as to why they should not attend family celebrations. 'You and I are all the family we need. We don't need them, Ramiro. We're happy, aren't we?'

But even as she would say that, Ramiro would see the sad, beaten down look on Darcia's face that had not changed since the day he met her. She seemed far from *happy*.

As Ramiro walked away from the house that morning, following a sleepless night on the porch after Darcia had thrown him out; all he could think of was that he should have listened to his family. Maybe they saw something in Darcia that he did not, as he had thought she was the answer to all his problems.

The divorce was bitter. Darcia made all sorts of false accusations about how Ramiro didn't spend enough time with her and the children, how he only thought of his family and didn't think of her. She refused to allow him contact with the children. Meanwhile, Ramiro had been staying in a rented flat with wallpaper peeling from the walls, electricity that kept cutting out, and only cold water, while Darcia lived in the house he had purchased with his hard-earned money.

His brother and sister had refused to help him after he'd cut them out of his life when he was busy pleasing Darcia. His mother had died the year before, and Ramiro had not even gone to her funeral because Darcia had refused to attend. She even threatened to leave him if he went, saying that his family had never really cared about him and she was the only one who did. Ramiro's father had left the country shortly after his mother died, retiring to Spain. Ramiro didn't even know his address.

Emily had been there for him throughout the bitter divorce. She had been like a light at the end of a very dark tunnel. She talked to him about how it was so easy to get into the wrong relationships. She told him all about her relationship with Russell and how badly he treated her. They planned a way out of everything. They would be together, and they would have their own family. So he could not understand what had made her change her mind about moving in with him. He hoped he would find that Russell had forced her to stay. That way, at least she hadn't lied to him, hadn't built him up just to knock him down, like Darcia had done.

Ramiro spent two hours just sitting in the car outside the flat that Emily shared with Russell, but no one came out.

He was about to get out of the car and knock the door, when it opened and a man walked out. *That must be Russell*, he thought, as a tall, skinny man with shoulder-length brown hair made his way along the garden path. He was carrying a brown box. The man stopped walking and looked ahead of him as if confused for a moment, then he appeared angry about something, talking to himself under his breath. The man turned and went back into the house.

After seeing that, Ramiro wondered whether it would be the wrong time to go and knock on the door. The man, whom he assumed was Russell, had appeared to be peeved about something.

Eventually, Ramiro decided he would have to go and ask about Emily. If he didn't, he would be forever wondering if she was there. He knew he would have to make up a story as to why he had come and who he was. His brain tried to think of something as he walked hesitantly towards the front door of the house.

The man who might be Russell opened the door.

'What?' he said as he looked at Ramiro with sunken, dark eyes.

'Um... Is Emily in?'

The man frowned. 'Who wants to know?'

'Um... my name is Frank, I'm a colleague from work. We had a collection when she was leaving and we wanted to give her the present, but she didn't turn up to the leaving do today. Is she at home?'

'No.'

'Oh... er, do you know when she'll be back?'

'To tell you the truth, Frank, I couldn't give a shit. She's run off again. She's always fucking running off when we have a row. She'll come back with her tail between her legs eventually. You can bring the present here and I'll give it to her when I see her. Bitch took my car this time.'

'Thank you,' said Ramiro, walking away.

So, she did leave him. But where did she go? He could not make sense of it. It felt like someone had stabbed his heart. She had been telling him the truth about wanting to leave Russell, but in the end, had she decided to break away on her own?

Ramiro went home and sat waiting all day, hopeful that Emily would come to him. But there was no word from her.

He went to work the next day. Maybe she had phoned someone at work. He chatted with her friend, Jill, in the hope that she would have some news, but Jill had not heard from Emily since the Friday before.

That evening, after returning home after work and still finding no sign of Emily, Ramiro decided to visit her parents' house. As he pulled up in his car outside their house, he saw a middle-aged man, whom he thought must be her father, happily pruning some roses. A woman emerged from the house with a cup of tea or coffee; her mother, he presumed. The couple laughed about something. Surely, if something had happened to Emily, they would not be looking so happy. His fears about her being involved in a car accident had been taunting him all night and all day after he found out that she had taken Russell's car.

At the same time, he felt duped. If Emily was okay but had simply cut her ties with him without an explanation, she was doing exactly what Darcia had done to him. He shrugged off his feelings of inadequacy.

He pondered their last few meetings. She hadn't talked much, and he'd got the impression that she wasn't sure about leaving Russell; but maybe she just wasn't sure about moving in with him.

He knew he would have to ask her parents if they'd heard from her. He took a deep breath and stepped out of his car.

'Hello, sorry to bother you,' he said as he approached them. 'I'm Ramiro, a friend of Emily's.'

He noticed the smile on Emily's mother's face fade. 'Hello,' she said, as if bracing herself for some bad news. 'Er... she did mention you when she phoned.' Her mother looked out into the street to the left and right as if trying to see something. Ramiro turned his head to see what she was looking at. Then he heard her say, 'Are you sure you should be here?'

He turned towards her and shrugged. 'Um... I just wanted to make sure she's okay. I haven't heard from her. She was supposed to come and stay with me but never arrived.'

Her mother's eyes widened. 'Oh,' was all she could say.

'Do you know where she's staying?' asked Ramiro, looking at her mother and seeing a blank expression. He turned to her father.

'We thought she was—' started her father.

'She's staying with a friend,' said her mother. Her cheeks were flushed and she appeared unable to meet his eyes.

Emily's father shook his head as if baffled.

'Um... do you have an address for her, please?' asked Ramiro.

'No, I'm afraid she doesn't want anyone to know where she is. I'm sure she'll be in touch when she's settled.' She looked at him sympathetically.

'Okay, well... when you speak to her, can you tell her I'd like to see her?'

'Of course,' said Emily's mother through gritted teeth.

Emily's parents looked at each other, knowingly, as Ramiro walked away.

'She never changes,' said her father, as Ramiro's car pulled away.

'Looks like she's broken that boy's heart,' said her mother, staring into the cup of coffee she had brought out for Emily's father.

'It's just like the last time she ran off after a row with Russell. She told you she was going to stay with her friend, Susan, but ended up lodging with that Australian fellow she met in a bar.' Emily's dad left the gardening behind and walked past her mother into the house.

'We'll have to wait until she decides it's time to get in touch. I hate this. She'll be the death of me that girl. I hardly slept last time not knowing where she was; then she breezes in after six weeks and acts as if she's never even been away.' Emily's mother's brow furrowed. 'Why is she like this? Her sisters are both so sensible.'

Ramiro drove away, perplexed, confused, and embarrassed that he'd gone to speak to her parents. He concluded that Emily had not been as serious about him as he was about her. She'd lied to him. Left him without a reason, just like Darcia had done. *Why do I get involved with these women?* He could not understand how she had so easily fooled him. Had he learnt nothing from his experience with Darcia? Was he destined to end up with the wrong women time and time again, constantly being used? He'd heard somewhere that if you don't learn from your mistakes, you'll repeat them over and over until you learn the lesson. Is that what this was? Some kind of test? He'd thought Emily was different. She had come across as being so honest, and when he had told her about what Darcia had done to him, she had been sympathetic.

She'd once said, 'Good people always end up with people who use them. Opposites attract, and all that. I just never thought it would happen to me. It's easy to take advantage of a good person. It's like the proverbial moth to the flame, we fall for it every time. Russell really fooled me.' Her eyes had been full to the brim with tears when she'd said that. Ramiro had felt that they were kindred spirits, both of them having been lied to by someone they had fallen for.

He thought he could trust Emily. *How will I ever know if someone is telling the truth or if they are just using me?* He remembered how her mother had said she'd mentioned him when she'd spoken to her on the phone. He regretted not asking what she'd said. But surely, if she'd had a message for him, her mother would have passed it on. *Why didn't she phone me?* he wondered. Then he recalled her mother saying, 'Are you sure you should be here?' What did that mean? Ramiro could feel his head splitting, just trying to make sense of it.

That evening, he put all of Emily's belongings in black bin bags and left them for the dustmen.

Chapter 11

Ramiro was afraid he would be locked up for murdering Emily. He could be in prison for years. A grey cell, no warmth, no freedom, fear surrounding his every waking hour. Cold sweat covered his brow. He sat in the police cell, shivering, more from fear than the temperature. He had never been in trouble with the police. He took a few deep breaths to calm his restless heart.

The police had visited him shortly after Emily's body was found. At first, they had just asked a few questions. They had also questioned Emily's boyfriend, Russell. Russell had an alibi; he had been working on the evening Emily was killed—well, police were assuming that she had been killed on the night she disappeared because the forensic investigation had concluded that her body had been decomposing for that amount of time. They'd let Russell go, although he was warned that he could still be called back if more evidence was found.

Ramiro felt sure that Russell had something to do with the murder. Russell was a criminal. Surely the police should lock him up for this crime anyway. It would be some justice to make up for all the other crimes he'd committed and got away with. Ramiro remembered how Emily had been afraid of Russell. He thought back to his one meeting with the man, when he had visited the flat looking for Emily; Russell looked like a drug addict. His eyes were hollow, devoid of emotion, as if he could just kill someone and not feel a thing. He felt a hatred towards Russell that he could hardly contain.

As he had been waiting for Emily on the night that she disappeared, Ramiro had been at home; he didn't have an alibi— the police seemed to be focusing more on him than Russell, solely for that reason. His head was splitting from the injustice of it all. He was racking his brain trying to remember whether anyone might have seen him go into his flat that night, or whether he had spoken to anyone. Then he remembered something and relief flooded his mind for a moment—his neighbour, Elsie Little, had asked him to help her change a light bulb that evening. She was a short woman, under five feet tall, and this particular ceiling was very high. Ramiro remembered that it had been about eight o' clock because he'd just finished watching *EastEnders* and had been in high spirits anticipating Emily's arrival at any moment. When Elsie had knocked on the door, he'd thought it was Emily. He'd flung open the front door and grinned widely. Then he looked down and saw Elsie Little standing there. His grin turned into a half-smile, painting the disappointment onto his face.

He had told Elsie that he was expecting Emily to visit, and said he would have to leave a note for her on the door so that she would know where he was. Ramiro went back inside his flat and found a piece of scrap paper. He wrote,

"Ems, I'm at Miss Little's flat, changing a light bulb. Back soon, Ramiro."

He stuck the note to the door with a piece of sticky tape and followed Miss Little to her flat. He must have been there for about 15 minutes. When he returned, the note was still on the door. He took it off, hoping that Emily had just left it there when she went into the flat, and that she would be inside waiting for him. But she was not.

As he thought back, he remembered that his friend, Brian, had phoned him that evening at about 9 p.m. to tell him something which he couldn't quite recall. He knew it had something to do with work, but couldn't remember what exactly. He remembered telling Brian that he was waiting for Emily. Would Brian remember that? Could he be a witness? That was two people at least; Miss Little and Brian. They could provide him with the alibi he needed. He began to feel calmer.

Ramiro's solicitor arrived half an hour later and told him that the police were ready to question him. Mr. Kirkpatrick, his solicitor, was also acting for him in relation to his divorce from Darcia, and in the application he had made for contact with his children. Darcia had been refusing to allow him to see the children, stating that he was now seeing a woman who was a drug addict. She had seen Emily with Ramiro only once, and when she saw Emily's bright red hair she had commented to Ramiro that she did not want her children associating with a "whore". She told him that the only access she was willing to allow would be supervised visits in a contact centre, provided he promised to attend on his own, without Emily.

As soon as Ramiro saw his solicitor, he was reminded of the bitter battle for contact with his children. He began to panic that if Darcia heard about him being questioned by the police, she would use it against him.

'There's not much we can do about that now, I'm afraid,' said Mr. Kirkpatrick, sighing. 'The Emily Baxter murder is national news, and your photo will probably be in the papers. I'm sorry. But, looking on the bright side, as long as we can prove you didn't—' The solicitor paused, his expression making it clear that he was unsure how to continue.

'You... You don't really believe that I had anything to do with this, do you?' Ramiro's eyes widened. If his solicitor doubted him, who would believe him? Everything was suddenly far more complicated. It would be an uphill battle. Some part of Ramiro wanted to scream out to the world that he was innocent, but he feared that no one would listen. The sweat began to form on his brow again as his heart beat faster.

'Don't worry, Ramiro. If you're innocent, we will get you out of this.'

If? Why had he said *if* as if he was unsure? 'Please, Mr. Kirkpatrick, you have to believe me,' pleaded Ramiro, as if he were addressing the judge and jury in the case, 'I loved Emily. There is no way I would have ever hurt her. It's that ex-boyfriend of hers. He did it, I'm sure of it.'

The solicitor sat down next to Ramiro on the bed in the cell. 'Do you have any evidence? Did Emily say anything to you that would have indicated that he could have killed her?'

'She was scared of him. I know that. He was taking drugs.'

'Your wife... er... I mean, Darcia, says that Emily was also on drugs.'

'I have already told you, that's not true. Emily was a good woman. She wanted to leave Russell because he was part of a gang. She was frightened. I really believe he killed her.' Ramiro was talking fast, as if hoping that just by saying this he could turn the tables in his favour and the police would go and arrest Russell.

'I can't use any of this, I'm afraid; it's all hearsay evidence. Did you ever come into contact with Russell Banks? Did he say anything to you that would make you think he murdered Emily?'

'No, I only met him once, after she disappeared. I went to the flat looking for her. He said she'd left him and taken his car.'

'Yes, that's what he told the police.' Mr. Kirkpatrick nodded.

Ramiro sighed deeply. 'I just know that he has something to do with it... if they search the flat where Emily was living, they'll find drugs. Emily said he is a dealer.'

'I'm sure the police will be searching the flat, but we need to concentrate on your defence, Mr. Lopez. The fact remains, Emily was on her way to see you when she disappeared. The police want to know the reasons behind that.'

Ramiro frowned. Nothing he had said had made a blind bit of difference. He was still at square one.

He somehow got through the two-hour police interview, but he felt more and more like a murder suspect with each question, and the way the police officers looked at him made him feel physically sick.

The police let him go free, just as they'd let Russell go—with the same warning that he would most likely be questioned again when more evidence was uncovered. Ramiro's solicitor frowned as he related the bad news: this turn of events would not help his application for contact with his children. Ramiro could do nothing but stare as his solicitor drove away. It had been months since he had been able to hug his children. He knelt down there in the police car park and let the tears fall.

* * *

The first day back at work after his police interview was one of the hardest days he had ever faced. His colleagues behaved as if they were almost afraid of him. Could they really be thinking that he had murdered Emily? They'd known about Ramiro and Emily's close friendship, and Jill was even aware that they had been planning to move in together shortly before Emily's disappearance. Before his arrest, his colleagues had been sympathetic, realising that Ramiro would be missing Emily. Jill, who had known about Emily's previous track record of running away, had felt sad for Ramiro; she'd comforted him. 'Don't worry,' she'd said, 'Emily will turn up. She probably just needs time to think.'

Now, suddenly, things had changed. His colleagues frowned at him where before there would have been sympathetic smiles; they avoided talking to him; they kept a distance, only speaking to him when it was absolutely necessary. He didn't know if he was being paranoid, but he would walk into a room and people would suddenly stop talking.

By the end of the day, Ramiro was dying to go home and get away from the tense atmosphere. He was even thinking that he might have to quit his job, but the job market was poor and he was worried about keeping up the rent payments on his flat. He was already having to pay quite a large chunk of his wage each month to his ex-wife for the children. He loved his children, but felt aggrieved that he was having to pay money for their welfare and yet was being denied access. He sometimes felt like breaking into his former home and taking the children away with him, disappearing somewhere. He hated Darcia and often harboured angry thoughts about her; fantasising about taking revenge for all the pain she had caused him. He found himself wishing she would die. Then he would remember Emily and he would be overcome by misery.

Thoughts such as these were clouding his mind as he made his way out of the office towards the car park. As he approached his car, he noticed that there were two men standing next to it. They were looking at him, and he began to feel intimidated by their stares. One of the men was standing in front of the driver's door. Ramiro wondered whether he should just turn around, go back to the office, and wait for them to go; but something told him that they were waiting for him. Were they plain-clothes police? Was he going to be arrested again? Their attire suggested that they were not policemen. One of the men was dressed in torn denim jeans. He had tattoos and a skinhead haircut. His face was adorned with many piercings.

The other man was taller, dressed all in black. Black leather trousers, a black hoodie. Lots of gold jewellery.

Ramiro looked behind him. It was quite dark, but there were other people in the car park, so he made up his mind to get into his car as quickly as possible and drive away.

As he approached his car, the man in denim said, 'Well, well, well, so this is the great Ramiro.'

Ramiro was taken aback. How did they know his name? 'Er... do I know you?' he said, almost under his breath.

'Make a habit of stealing other men's girlfriends, do you?' said the other man.

'Er... I don't know what you mean,' said Ramiro. He had now stopped walking and was considering running back to the office, but he feared that these men would be able to catch him. He looked behind him again, hoping to see someone he knew. The car park seemed suddenly empty.

'Give me your car keys,' said the leather-clad man.

Ramiro was now trembling, but felt slightly relieved. *Perhaps all they want is the car?* he thought. He reached into his jacket pocket, and pulled out the car keys. As he passed them to the man, the keys jangled in his shaking hand. Ramiro then turned to leave.

He felt an arm grab him. 'Where do you think you're going?' he heard the skinhead say.

The man pulled him towards the car. Ramiro thought of shouting for help, but worried that these men might be armed.

Soon he was bundled into the boot of his car, enveloped in darkness as the lid was shut on him, forcing his legs into an awkward position. He could hear laughter as the men slammed the doors shut and the engine began to purr. Ramiro tried to find a comfortable position, his knees were up against his chin, and with every bump in the road, his spine felt like it would snap. He could hear the muffled words of the men in the car. He was sure they had said the name *Russ*. So, this was about Emily. His throat became tight, breathing more difficult. He remembered his meeting with Russell just after Emily had gone missing. A flashback of Russell's hollow eyes caused him to fear for his life. He felt sure that Russell and these two thugs had something to do with Emily's murder, and now, they were probably planning a similar fate for him.

After an uncomfortable journey, the car came to a halt and Ramiro heard the car doors open and close as his two captors exited.

Shortly, the boot was opened and Ramiro gasped, thankful to finally be breathing some fresh air. He was hoisted out of the car and dropped onto the ground like a roll of carpet.

'Here he is, boss,' he heard one of the two men say.

Ramiro slowly found his bearings, and, with great pain and difficulty, straightened himself out and stood up. He was face to face with Russell Banks.

Looking to his left, he saw a cliff edge and the sprawling ocean below.

'The criminal always returns to the scene of the crime,' said Russell.

As Ramiro pulled his eyes away from the imposing sea view, his thoughts cascaded: *What does he mean: the criminal always returns to the scene of the crime? Is this where he killed Emily? Why are we here? He's going to ki... kill me, too...*

Russell approached Ramiro and grabbed him by the collar. 'You were having an affair with my girlfriend, making me look like an idiot. No one gets away with doing something like that to Russell Banks.'

'She... She told me you had split up.'

Russell pushed him so that he fell backwards onto the ground. 'Don't lie to me, you fucking wanker.' He leaned over Ramiro. 'You knew I was still living with Emily because you came to the flat after she went missing... remember that, Ramiro? Or should I call you "Frank"? You fucking lied to me saying your name was Frank, why should I believe a fucking word you say now? Think it's funny to steal another man's bird, then try to make a fucking fool of them, do you?'

'I... She said you were seeing someone else,' said Ramiro. 'Look, I thought you two were over. I would never have—'

'I don't care!' shouted Russell. 'Stand up!'

Ramiro scrambled to his feet. He was faced with Russell, looking at him as if he wanted him dead, and the two thugs—one on either side of him—looking thirsty for blood.

'So, why did you kill Emily?' asked Russell.

'I didn't kill her. I swear to you. I loved Emily.'

'So, what happened then?'

'I don't know. She was supposed to be meeting me at my flat, but she didn't turn up. Th... That's why I came looking for her at your flat.'

'So why did you feel the need to lie about your fucking name when you met me? You obviously didn't want me to know who you were 'cos you knew you were screwing her behind my back... You knew me and her were still together.'

'No... No... She said—'

'Oh shut up, Ramiro! If you weren't sticking your nose into my relationship, this would never have happened. Emily would still be alive if you weren't involved. Yeah, we were going through a rough patch, but she needed me. You filled her head with romantic shit, and she left me. Why did you think you had the right to take another man's girl? You are to blame for her death, Ramiro. *You.*'

Russell poked Ramiro in the chest with his forefinger when he said "you". It was very dark, and hard for Ramiro to make out any of the expressions on Russell's face. But he knew he was angry. His voice was getting louder and deeper.

'Let's make a deal,' said Russell. 'Let's not pretend that I actually give a shit about Emily dying; in fact, you did me a favour. She was so needy. So self-righteous. Always nagging, moaning. She never appreciated me. Got what she deserved, if you ask me. Now, I want you to do one more thing for me, and I'll let you go instead of throwing you off this cliff to join your beloved whore.'

The two men behind Russell laughed.

Russell appeared annoyed at this. He turned to face them, fire in his eyes. 'I don't pay you to fucking laugh. This is fucking serious.' He approached the man in black, stealthily, like a lion sizing up its prey.

Ramiro tried to think about how he could escape. There was a window of opportunity here. The adrenaline rushed through him causing him to shake involuntarily.

'You don't pay us, Russ. Stevo does,' said the man in denim, almost as an aside.

Russell turned his attention to the denim-clad man, his eyes narrowed. 'You trying to be clever, or something? Stevo sent you to help me; you don't get paid if you don't help me. Comprendez?' He had his face inches from the skinhead's face.

Ramiro began to walk backwards. *If I can just get far enough away while they're arguing, I can make a run for it.*

Suddenly, things changed. The man in black looked over at Ramiro. 'He's trying to get away, boss.'

All three men were upon Ramiro before he had a chance to think. The two thugs dragged him up from the ground where he had fallen, grabbing hold of one arm each. When he was upright, Russell stared into his eyes, and with sour breath spat in his face as he said, 'You try anything like that again and I'll set these two on you. They may look like fools but they can do more damage than a pack of rottweilers.'

'What do you mean "fools"?' said the tattooed man.

'Oh, shut up!' shouted Russell. He began to pace around as if he'd lost his mind. Then quite suddenly, he stopped in front of them and said, 'This is serious. I won't have any more lip from you two hoodlums. Emily might have been a whore, but she was my whore and I'm the only one who gets to call her that. I'm the one she betrayed, not you. Have some respect for the dead, or you'll be joining her soon.'

The two men bowed their heads, in an almost simultaneous response.

'Now, where was I? Oh yeah, I was gonna throw you off the cliff, wasn't I? It would be quite poetic, almost like Romeo and Juliet, really,' he said with an eerie grin and unfocused eyes as he poked Ramiro in the chest. The two men gripped Ramiro's arms tighter and he imagined being hurled over the cliff edge, the vertigo turning his stomach.

'Okay, take that as a warning. Now, back to business,' said Russell rubbing his hands together. 'I've got the bloody pigs sniffing around me now because they think I had something to do with Emily's murder. I can't afford to have them too close; it gets in the way of my work. This goes no further, Ramiro, or I'll hunt you down and this time, you will be going off that cliff, you hear me?'

Ramiro nodded.

'I deal in drugs, in stolen goods. If the pigs find out, they'll mess everything up. Bitch was driving the stolen car when she was murdered; she landed me right in it. Now the pigs wanna search my flat. I'm having to get rid of all the crack. A couple of the gang have backed up my story about where I got the car, but it's not watertight. If that falls apart, the pigs are gonna be seriously trying to frame me for the murder. They wanna close their files; they don't like loose ends. It's not good for their statistics. I've spent years building up my contacts and I don't need this shit. So... I've come up with a plan that'll benefit both of us.' He shifted his gaze to the two men standing either side of Ramiro. 'You don't have to keep holding him, you numbskulls. Ramiro knows a good deal when he hears it. He won't try and run away again. Give the man some breathing space.'

The two men let go of his arms and even after they let go he could still feel the tension of their grip as the blood tried to find its way back to his upper arms. The men stood either side of him like guardsmen.

'You're gonna go to the pigs,' continued Russell, 'and confess to killing Emily. That'll get 'em off my back. You say you had an argument that got out of hand and she fell off the cliff or something... I'll leave the details to you.' He smiled as he spoke, eyes wide, as if he were proposing a fun day out. 'You'll get locked up for a few years, manslaughter or something. When you're out, you come and find me and I'll make sure you're looked after. You can come and work for me. I'll give you a split of the profits. What d'you say?'

Ramiro stood, stock still, unable to believe what was being asked of him. 'But... I didn't kill Emily.'

'You know that, I know that, hey, even the man upstairs knows that. Don't worry, nothing bad'll happen to you.'

'But the real killer gets away.'

'Well, yeah. But I don't really care about that. So, will you or won't you, Ramiro?' He grabbed Ramiro by the shoulders and turned him towards the cliff to look out at the water.

'If you don't agree to my plan, you get to follow Emily. I won't feel sorry about reuniting you either. You deserve each other.'

'You don't understand,' said Ramiro, 'I have two children. My wife won't let me see them. If I go into prison I will lose them for ever.' Tears filled his eyes.

Russell stood in front of him, his stare boring deep into Ramiro's eyes: 'Well, you should've thought of that before stealing another man's girl, shouldn't you?'

Emily had told Ramiro she was pregnant and that the child was his. He'd mourned the death of both of them. But this was hardly the time or place to say anything about that now. He could almost feel the fire burning out from Russell's eyes; the man looked ready to murder someone.

'Okay, okay, I'll do it.' Ramiro was shaking, a million thoughts swimming around his mind. Would the two thugs stay with him and make sure he goes to the police station, or would he have time to escape? He could go into hiding, change his name.

'You have until tomorrow evening, shall we say 8 p.m.?' Russell's deep voice interrupted his thoughts. 'If you haven't confessed by then, we're coming back here.' Russell pulled Ramiro nearer to the cliff edge and held his shoulders. 'Look at that sea. Beckoning. Emily's soul is out there.' He laughed eerily.

Ramiro shrugged to loosen Russell's grip, then turned towards him. Russell sneered as he removed his hands from his shoulders. 'My two friends will come home with you and accompany you to the station tomorrow.'

Russell stood with his back to the cliff edge as he spoke. Ramiro felt an urge and before he could think twice, he pushed Russell with all his strength, wanting to make sure he would fall off the cliff edge. Russell tried to resist, but he fell backwards, a scream filling the air. The momentum drove Ramiro forward and he lost his footing on the cliff edge, rolling forward and banging his head on a rock before plummeting down after Russell.

Ramiro's body was found on the shore a few days later. The newspapers began to speculate about whether he was guilty of killing Emily and whether he had returned to the scene of the murder to commit suicide.

Russell's body was never found, leaving police wondering whether he had fled the country when they tried to locate him for further questioning.

The media ran stories for the next few months with a debate ensuing as to whether Ramiro or Russell was the guilty party. No conclusion was reached either way. Nigel received a running commentary on all of this from June, who apparently found the mystery more enthralling than the soap operas she liked to watch on TV.

Fifteen years after the incident, one of the two stooges appeared on a *Panorama* special. At that time, he was a reformed criminal, and his identity was hidden from the public. He appeared on television in darkness, an actor's voice speaking his words. 'I was there on that day... Russell and Ramiro were fighting... they both fell from the cliff. It was an accident.' Following this exclusive revelation, the police were back at square one. There was no proof that either man was responsible for the murder of Emily Baxter; in fact, from the informant's version of events, it appeared that neither man had murdered her. He had recalled Russell asking Ramiro why he had killed her, and Ramiro saying, 'I didn't kill Emily'. The circumstances surrounding her death remained a mystery.

Chapter 12

'Isabella, stop fighting with your brother! You're older than him; you should know better!'

'He was the one who took my colouring pencils!' Isabella stood with her hands on her hips. Her brown eyes stared at her mother and she wore the frown that so reminded Darcia of Ramiro. He'd always had a frown on his face as far as she could recall. When they'd first met, he'd had a frown on his face. That was one of the things that had endeared him to her.

She shook herself out of her reverie. 'Oh, go and play in your room! I want to watch the news.'

'But I want to watch TV!'

'Go to your room!' Darcia shouted, louder than she had intended. She knew she would have to find a way of reining in her anger. She always overreacted, almost frightening the children with her words whenever one of them looked at her in a way that reminded her of Ramiro. They had both inherited his dark looks. Darcia had been happy about that once. She'd always hated her own pale complexion and mousy brown hair. Ramiro was very handsome; that much she had to admit, even in her most vengeful mood.

As Isabella ran upstairs, followed by her brother, a spark of guilt hit Darcia again as it often did when she thought of how she had left Ramiro, depriving the children of a loving father. He had been a doting, caring father. She could not have wished for a better father for her children; but that was just it—she'd chosen Ramiro for his looks. She knew he would bear good-looking children. He had served his purpose, and she could no longer bear to live with him. She had never loved him.

Before Ramiro, she had lived with Dennis, a man who drained the very lifeblood from her. She had met Dennis when she was just seventeen years old and was eager for romance. He told her she was the most beautiful girl he'd ever met. He took her out to expensive restaurants, bought her luxurious gifts, and whisked her away on romantic weekends. He used to talk about the day they would get married and start a family. He told her everything he knew she wanted to hear. This went on for almost a year before she found out the truth: Dennis was already married and he had at least one other mistress that she knew about. Moreover, Dennis was not going to let anything break up his marriage. He'd married into money, which was how he'd afforded to keep mistresses. He didn't want to lose that.

When Darcia threatened to tell his wife about his affairs, he called her a slut and arranged for three of his friends to warn her off by following her home one night and dragging her into a disused warehouse. Once inside, they described to her in detail what they would do to her if she ever told. She feared for her life.

After scaring the living daylights out of her for over an hour, the three brutes let her go, but one of the men, Tom, followed her and tried to persuade her to go home with him. He became very angry when she refused, and he slapped her across the face.

Dennis still very much thought of Darcia as his property, so when he saw her the next day, he wanted to know where she got the black eye and cut lip. When she told him, he didn't believe her and insisted they go and confront the man together.

When they arrived at the council estate where Tom lived, he was in the process of injecting himself with something. He thanked Dennis for giving him the money for the drugs and asked if there were any other favours he could do for him, winking at Darcia.

She flinched.

'Did you do this to her?' screamed Dennis.

'She asked for it,' said the drugged-up Tom.

'I paid you to frighten her, not to batter her. I have a right mind to ask for my money back.'

'Sorry, boss, it's gone.' He smiled and revealed the gaps where three of his front teeth should have been.

'Let's go,' said Darcia, creeped out by the hovel with flickering lights, peeling wallpaper, and the distinct scent of urine in the air.

As they walked away from the block of flats, Darcia turned to Dennis. 'How do you even know someone like that?'

'That's where I used to live, before I met my wife. That's why I can't risk going back.'

Darcia shivered. 'Look, I won't tell her about us. Den, I think we should call it a day. We've had some good times, but now I know about your other women—'

'If that's what you want,' he said shrugging.

She sighed with relief.

'But there's one thing you need to know. I know a lot of criminals. If you make me angry, you will pay. I know murderers, rapists, blood-hungry types.' He spun around and grabbed her shoulders. 'I decide when it's over, okay?'

'But... But...'

His hands were gripping her arms so tightly, she feared the blood supply would be affected. 'You have other women. I thought it was just me and you...'

'You're the only one I care about,' he said.

'But you're married.'

'I married her for the money. How else d'you think I'd afford to buy you so many things?'

Darcia sighed. 'Let go of my arms. You're hurting me.'

He let go and began picking his nails in a nervous motion.

'If you care about me so much, why did you just threaten to hurt me? And you got those men to threaten me last night and you've just said that if I leave you, you'll set your criminal friends on me.'

He looked her in the eye. 'That's because you're mine.'

She tore her eyes away from his stare. 'You're scaring me.'

'Darcie.' He stroked her hair gently with his hand. 'Just forget about the other women and let's go back to how we were before you found out.'

'How... How can I do that? You're married and have another mistress, and now I also know you're associated with criminals.'

'Yes, but don't you see? Now I don't have to lie to you anymore. I hated lying to you.'

'Okay, so how many other women are there?'

'Just Angie and Jane.'

'Your wife and mistress?' She sighed. 'If you love me so much, how come you've got another mistress?'

'She had my child, so I have to look after her.'

Darcia pushed his hand away from her hair. 'It's over, Den. I can't live like this.' She walked away quickly, but something landed on her head. He had hit her with a large piece of wood.

She woke up later in her flat, with a terrible pain in her head. He was there but he refused to call an ambulance, saying he had a criminal record and didn't want to be found out.

So, from the age of eighteen, Darcia became almost a slave to Dennis. She was stuck with him. She couldn't leave for fear of the repercussions, but she hated being with him. For over five years, she remained in the relationship, always at his beck and call. He spent most of his time with her, somehow sensing that she was keen to find a way to leave him. She lived for the times when he would go and see his wife or his other mistress, when she could feel some peace of mind, even if it was short-lived.

She was saved from the situation when, one night, Dennis got into a fight with one of his criminal friends but didn't live to tell the tale. Darcia was free, but she was the shell of the person she had once been; no longer able to look herself in the mirror, feeling angry all the time. It took her ten years to get back to some sort of normalcy, but she promised never to let a man close to her ever again.

When she was in her mid thirties, she began to feel that she didn't fit in. All her friends were starting families, and she thought that having children would give her purpose in life. That was when she met Ramiro and set about her plan to have his children and leave him. She could never love a man again, never wanted to be shackled in a relationship. Every time Ramiro touched her, it reminded her of Dennis, and she wanted so badly to be free. She did *try* to change her attitude; she knew Ramiro was a good man. There were no skeletons in his closet waiting to pounce. Yet even knowing that, she could not bear to live with him. So he had to go.

Darcia flicked over the TV channel to watch the news. She recognised the picture on the screen as Chelsea Beach, where a young girl's body had been discovered not too long ago, and she recalled how Ramiro had been questioned about his relationship with the girl. Darcia knew Ramiro could never murder anyone, but she'd used the information against him in her legal documents as a reason why Ramiro should not be allowed to have contact with the children. She knew she was wrong to have done that, but she didn't allow emotions to guide her. She had to make sure she stayed in control and that Ramiro could not dictate what happened to the children.

"The body of Ramiro Lopez was found just a few hundred yards from where Emily Baxter's body was discovered..."

Darcia's mouth fell open and she began to shake her head. 'No, this can't be true...' she said to herself. 'I must have heard it wrong...'

"...early indications seem to point to suicide being the cause of death. There are suggestions that if Ramiro was perhaps feeling guilty over the death of his former lover, he may have committed suicide. However, the police have asked us to stress that that they have not concluded enquiries into her death. The Emily Baxter case is very much still open. However, with the death of Ramiro Lopez occurring so close in time, and at the same beach, it has caused speculation. There is even talk of a possible suicide pact

between the couple. Various lines of enquiry are now being looked into."

Darcia was gripped by a tormented surge of guilt that tore through her. Only last week, she had indicated to Ramiro through her solicitors that she was thinking of stopping all contact between him and the children. Could that have been what pushed him over the edge? She knew he was not capable of murder... so there must have been another reason for him to decide to end it all...

The woman who had not felt true emotion in almost twenty years now began to cry. Her tears fell silently on a face that was stiff. Her mind was repeating: *Sorry, Ramiro; sorry, Ramiro... I'm so sorry, Ramiro...*

Chapter 13

'Nigel, we have to talk,' said June as he walked past the living room doorway on his way to the kitchen. He had heard the *Crimewatch* theme tune when he walked through the front door.

'I'm going to the kitchen to eat something. I've had a long day,' he mumbled. He never hurried to get home. His working hours were 9.30 to 5.30, and if he caught the 6 p.m. train, he'd usually be home sometime after 7 pm, but he always stayed at work until 6.30, mainly reading books. He had discovered books as a young boy, when his parents seemed too caught up in their own lives to care about his. Books were the one thing that they didn't mind him taking an interest in. Had they encouraged his reading, though, he would have probably stopped reading, as he had grown to despise his parents. He'd somehow fallen into a pattern of reading all by himself, after discovering his school library and then it became almost an obsession until his teenage years when music and girls had taken over. Since he'd killed Emily, he found himself unable to control his thoughts, and he needed something that could help. He'd picked up a book one day to stop the overwhelming black thoughts that were making his life unbearable. He found that after reading a few pages, he could concentrate, at least partially, on the book's words, and less and less on the words that were floating around his head, reminding him of the murder. Reading, to him, represented a security blanket of sorts, taking him back to days when he didn't have to be in control, when everything was done for him. It had been an escape in his childhood, and he desperately needed an escape now. His concentration was limited, but he found that if he tried very hard, he could sometimes make the words on the pages of the novels and stories he read take precedence over those that were slowly tearing his mind apart. So, he joined a library and tried to read as often as he could to distract himself from all else.

Each evening after work, he would read for an hour or so, and slowly his childhood obsession made a reappearance. It was a way, too, of avoiding spending time with June. He would tell her that he had to work late, but really he was killing time. He would catch the late train and get home after 9 p.m., and tell June he was tired, as an excuse to be alone.

They never talked, so he felt nervous at the thought that June had said she wanted to talk to him tonight; he desperately wanted to avoid it. 'I thought you wanted to watch this,' he said, pointing to the television. *Crimewatch* was in full swing.

He turned to walk away towards the kitchen.

'No, wait, Nigel.' She stood up and switched off the television. 'You can eat after I've said what I have to say.'

He noticed she'd called him *Nigel*, rather than *Nige*, and felt a sense of foreboding that this was not going to be a friendly conversation. He stood in the doorway and the thought crossed his mind, as it did regularly, that June had finally discovered the part he'd played in Emily's death. Had he talked in his sleep? His nightmares were so vivid that he was always amazed June had never heard him scream; it all seemed to be lodged so deep inside his mind, tormenting him only. But maybe June had heard the screams, maybe they weren't all in his mind; maybe she'd just never said anything before.

June was looking at the floor. Frowning. Just when he thought she may have changed her mind about saying whatever it was that she had wanted to say, she sighed and looked up at him, her lips pursed, her brow creased. 'Come in and sit down,' she said as she sat back down on the sofa where she had been seated when he'd arrived.

He walked into the room cautiously and sat down beside her, avoiding her eyes.

'What I'm going to say isn't easy,' she started.

Fear gripped him. *She knows.*

'I've been to see a solicitor,' she continued.

Oh my God. Now I'm definitely going to prison. He imagined a cold cell, the walls bare, stark; a hollow room, bars, a locked door; no escape, no way out. Beads of sweat formed on his forehead. He'd waited for this moment. He knew he should be grateful. It would be a way to pay for what he had done. This would make it easier. He gulped and took a deep breath, staring at June as she continued:

'The kids have grown up now. Toby has been packed off to university. He won't need us anymore. Annabelle is living with Eric. I won't lie to you; I've only stayed with you to make it easier on the children. I knew that as soon as they grew up I'd have to leave you. I'm filing for divorce. My solicitor is preparing the papers.'

Nigel's eyes widened. He lived with the constant fear that one day, he'd say something, admit his guilt; it would all spill out and he'd be unable to control it. So he'd hardly spoken to his wife. He should not feel shocked by this revelation—he knew that—but somehow, he was. June had been the only dependable person in his life. He thought she'd always be there.

'Don't look at me like that.' June looked away from him and stared at her hands, fiddling with her nails, chipping away at bits of the dark red nail polish that was peeling away at the edges.

Nigel's eyes watched her fingers. The colour reminded him of blood... the blood on his hands. He felt himself tremble and pulled his eyes away.

'This marriage died a long time ago,' said June, matter-of-factly. Then she stood up and walked towards the door.

Nigel twisted around to look at her. She turned back towards him, and he saw the lines on her face etched through all the years she'd stood by, watching him deteriorate; staying with him through a false sense of duty, because of the children. At that moment, he realised that he had not only murdered one woman in this life. He had murdered his wife's very soul.

With a selfish sense of looking back, making sure he wasn't caught for a violent crime, he'd neglected his marriage and his children. He'd only had enough time for his constant regret about the murder. He'd allowed June to play a mothering role towards him. While he battled with his conscience through his depression and breakdown, she had been living a shadow of a life with a man who didn't even see her—a man too caught up in his own crazy world. Now it had ended. He had taken her for granted. But he also knew the truth: she'd have left him sooner, years before—twenty years before—if she knew what he had done. He had lied to her constantly by staying silent.

'I'm sorry, Nigel, but you'll have to move out. The solicitor says I will be able to stay in the house.'

Nigel remained silent, staring. There was nothing he could say in his defence. Eventually, as she turned to walk away, he asked in a tiny voice, 'Where will I go?'

June shook her head and shrugged, tears threatening to fall. 'You have to move out,' she said as she walked away.

Chapter 14

Nigel moved out a week later. Few words were said between him and June. There was nothing more to say. The only explanation he had for his behaviour was something he could never reveal. How could he tell her that the reason he had been so withdrawn from their relationship—from life—was because he had killed a woman in a fit of rage twenty years before, and his every waking moment since had been swallowed up by remorse, guilt, fear. He'd been too busy looking behind, keeping his head down, covering up, to pay attention to the life that passed him by each day. His children had grown up without his support. He had kept a distance from them, feeling unworthy of their love. His relationship with them was effectively non-existent, as if he had been an absent father. His body was there, but it was an empty shell. He lived alone inside his mind. The torturous memories encased him; a barrier to the outside world.

When he found himself out on the street at the age of fifty-five, the only home he'd known no longer a place he was welcome, he could think of no friends who would be willing to put him up. He could not call in any favours. He hadn't kept in touch with relatives. The fewer people he came into contact with, the less chance there was of anyone discovering his secret; that's how he'd lived. Now that he would have welcomed a friendly face, there were none.

Even his job was a lonely one. He worked alone in the basement of a large office building, for a legal firm. He was the man responsible for photocopying documents, posting the mail, and ordering stationary. After his breakdown, he found he could not return to his old line of work anymore. Computers had changed in the years since he'd been out of the job market. He'd settled for a low-key administration job, something that didn't require much concentration. He found that he'd all but lost that skill.

After moving out of the family home, Nigel decided to rent a flat in London near his workplace; that way he wouldn't have to commute. It was a small studio flat, but it was all he could afford.

His days were now mostly spent alone. He hardly came into contact with other people. The only people he saw were a few neighbours he passed on his way to work and the handful of staff who would enter his office to ask for photocopies or to bring him the office mail for franking and posting.

He likened his life to being in a prison. The twelve-foot square room in which he worked was painted white and only had two photocopiers and a couple of large tables, apart from his desk and a chair. He had a computer so that he could deal with internal e-mails, and a telephone so he could call out to place orders for office supplies. There was only one window in the room and that was very high up the wall. He could only see other buildings through that window. There was not much of a view at all.

The people he helped each day would sometimes stop to chat about the weather or news headlines, occasionally they would try and fail to have a conversation with him, but mostly they only stopped to give him instructions to photocopy this, or post that, or order this. There were no real friendships made in that place, even after he'd been working there for over sixteen years. It was a lonely existence.

He often thought about quitting his job; the time alone, the tedious mundane nature of it, left him with too much time to think. All he did was think. His thoughts were dark, reflecting his inner turmoil. More recently, thoughts of ending it all had become increasingly frequent.

About two weeks after Nigel had moved into his new flat, he decided to go and eat dinner one evening at a local café. He was sick of staring at four walls, of being alone, devoid of human contact.

On his way to the café, he noticed a young girl, perhaps in her late twenties. She was maybe three or four months pregnant, judging by the size of her stomach protruding from a tight-fitting top on an otherwise slender frame. Her hair was bright red. Nigel thought of pillar boxes, telephone kiosks, and wondered that there were not so many about nowadays. He felt saddened for a moment contemplating that they might disappear from the London streets for good one day; such iconic images of London, as recognisable as the London bus.

When he looked beyond the bright red of her hair, he caught his breath as he remembered Emily Baxter. As this girl walked past him, she smiled in his direction; he noticed her deep brown eyes. Memories flooded his mind, and he felt hot. Droplets of perspiration gathered on his brow. He turned around and watched her walk away. It was like seeing an image from the past, a flashback; but she was real, a human being that reminded him so much of Emily.

Of course, over the years, he had often noticed young pregnant women, feeling that tug of remorse, guilt, shame, each time he saw a woman with similar hair, or a similar face. Somehow this girl had brought all of that together; she had so many of Emily's qualities, it was uncanny.

He was unable to sleep that night. The thoughts invading his mind were like bullets coming hard and fast, causing him to feel actual pain. Seeing that look-alike had brought it all back to him vividly and made it all seem so real again. Not that he had ever been able to forget; it was always there lurking ready to pounce. Eventually, he took some sleeping pills and drifted off into a fitful sleep.

Chapter 15

The next day at work, Nigel had just walked into his office after making himself a cup of coffee in the staff kitchen. A girl stood in his room, holding a document file—nothing unusual about that, but what was unusual was that this was the same girl he had seen the evening before. The Emily Baxter look-alike. It was almost enough to make him spill the coffee onto his desk. His hands shook as he placed his cup onto the place mat.

'Hi,' said the girl. 'Are you Nigel?'

He had been holding his breath, so when he tried to speak he took a gulp of air, almost choking on it. He coughed and reddened. His back was turned towards her. He slowly twisted around. 'Ye... Yes,' he said, eyes down, afraid of catching her eye and bringing back those memories again. Paranoia gripped him, and fear caused sweat to creep across his brow. 'Wh... Who are you?' He stumbled on his words.

'I'm Kelly,' she said.

Nigel had half expected her to say "Emily Baxter". The sense of relief was enormous.

Kelly tossed back her red hair and smiled brightly, holding out her free hand to shake his.

He reached out and shook her hand with his sweaty palm and watched as she surreptitiously wiped her hand on her skirt.

'I've been sent here for some photocopies. Am I in the right room?' She looked around her, and her eyes settled on the two photocopiers at the far side of the small office.

'Yes.' When she turned to face him again, he held out his hand, his eyes fixed on the file in her hands, avoiding her face. He began to feel claustrophobic, and he worried that he might keel over.

'Er... I need ten copies of this bundle of documents, please,' she said. 'Can you call me when it's ready? It's quite urgent.'

'Ye... Yes... okay,' he said, nervously taking the file from her. He watched as she walked out of the room.

Nigel placed the bundle of papers on the photocopier and the following ten minutes or so passed by in a blur. He remembered taking the papers out of the file and placing them on the machine to be copied and even setting it up so that ten copies could be printed. After that, though, up until the copies were done and the whirring of the machine stopped, he had been lost in his thoughts. It was almost as if he had left his body and transcended somewhere else as the photocopier chugged away, spitting out duplicates of the papers that Kelly had given him to copy.

Seeing Kelly had been like meeting Emily again... but Emily was dead... and Kelly was young. He couldn't help wondering whether Emily had had any children. He could not remember reading anything about that in the news reports that followed her death, but then again he had mostly avoided reading those and had only been kept in the loop by June and her constant commentary about the case as more details were released by the police and the press.

Maybe Kelly was related to Emily in some way. How ironic that would be.

His mind awoke from its wanderings when the photocopier stopped and the ten copies were done. Kelly had asked him to call her when they were ready, but he did not recall whether she had given him her extension number.

Maybe the documents would give him some clue as to which department she worked in, he mused. He picked up one of the bundles and flicked through. His eyes widened as he saw for the first time what the documents were. When Kelly had handed the file to him and even when he'd taken the papers out of the file to place them on the photocopier, he had not been paying attention to the content. To his horror, all of the papers were copies of news stories from the national press about murders. One headline read: "Unsolved Crimes: Can New DNA Methods Help To Find The Perpetrators?", another said: "Getting Away With Murder: A

Psychological Study Into A Criminal Mind," another was entitled, "Can Murder Ever Be Forgiven?"

Nigel trembled then took a deep breath. An Emily Baxter double comes into his office with a folder of papers about murder. It was just a coincidence, a frightful one, but a coincidence just the same, he told himself.

He tried to make light of it: the company often held seminars and talks about legal issues; that was probably what these documents related to. He took a few document wallets out of his desk drawer and placed the new copies inside, wanting to cover them up so he couldn't see them. He still felt none the wiser as to which department Kelly could possibly work for. Just then, the door to his office opened and in walked Kelly.

'Me again,' she said brightly. 'I realised that I didn't give you my extension number, so I thought I'd better come down and get the papers. Are they ready?'

'Er... yes,' he said, in a daze. He handed her the files, eager to be parted from them, and he watched as she walked out of the door.

Chapter 16

As Nigel stepped out of the office building that evening, his mobile phone began to ring. Looking at the phone, he saw his daughter's name flashing. This was the first time she had phoned him since he'd left home. He felt a pang of guilt as he realised that he hadn't tried to get in touch with her.

For the past few weeks, he'd been feeling sorry for himself, wallowing in his pain. Every spare moment had been used trying to find somewhere to live after moving out of the marital home. He realised with remorse that he had not really even thought about his children during that time. It was a pattern; the reason June had asked him to leave. He had driven a wedge between himself and his family while he tried to cope with his guilt, constantly caught up in the misery of his regret for long periods of time. When he left home, part of him had expected he'd never see them again and he was ashamed to admit that along with the heartache at the thought came a smidgeon of relief.

He tried to remember the last time he had spoken to his daughter. He couldn't.

'Hello, Annabelle,' he said, trying to sound cheery as he answered the phone.

'Dad. Hi. I just heard the news about you and Mum. Me and Eric were away.'

'Right,' he said, not really knowing what to say.

'Mum wasn't going to tell me; she said she didn't want to worry me, but when me and Eric visited last week, there was a "For Sale" sign up. Is it really necessary to sell the house? House prices have plummeted. I think you're being selfish making Mum sell now. You should let her live there until the market recovers.'

'It was your mother's decision,' said Nigel, desperation in his voice.

'No. Mum said you've told her to sell—'

'The divorce, I mean... I didn't want it.'

There was silence on the line. Then his daughter spoke, in a slower and quieter tone. 'You can't blame this on Mum. She told me about you... Well, you weren't really fair on her, were you?'

Nigel's deepest, darkest secret had found its way into the light and he felt humiliated. Well, not *the* deepest, but the one that came a close second. He didn't want to discuss his sex life with his daughter. The truth was, Nigel had become so locked up within his own mind that it seemed his other bodily functions were affected. His doctor had sent him for various tests, given him pills to take, but he felt ashamed, as if he were less of a man. The real reason was psychological: *'Have you suffered a trauma of some kind?'* one of the young doctors at the hospital had asked him. *'Sometimes, if something really upsetting happens, it can shut down certain parts of the mind.'* Of course, Nigel had denied any traumatic occurrences and had just asked the doctor whether his nervous breakdown could have made him impotent. *'Yes,'* the doctor nodded thoughtfully, *'but, Mr Price, nervous breakdowns don't usually happen without some kind of trigger... There is always some reason for a breakdown. Are you sure you don't want to talk about things that might be bothering you? I could refer you to a counsellor.'* Nigel had, of course, refused.

When Nigel first became impotent a few months after his breakdown, June was offended. It seemingly came out of the blue that he could no longer perform in the bedroom. She suspected he was seeing someone else, or that he didn't find her attractive her anymore. It caused no end of rows. First they rowed about the problem itself, but in the end they ignored that and would argue about any other trivial matter. Well, in truth, it was June who had done all the arguing, Nigel would for the most part sit and listen, chirping in now and then in a restrained voice, holding back his true feelings. He could not let his anger out again. This relative silence on his part annoyed June even more, and she began to believe that he just didn't care anymore.

Nigel had been oblivious to June's moods most of the time, trying his hardest to keep his sanity and shut out the constant voice in his head reminding him that he was a *murderer...* *murderer... murderer...* It never stopped.

After what must have been a few months, June seemed to switch off, too. It had been over eighteen years since they made love; the last time had probably been when they had conceived their son, Toby.

Nigel often wondered whether by stemming his natural angry feelings, he had also affected the flow of testosterone. Anger was linked to testosterone levels, wasn't it? And so was arousal. But he could not and would not allow the anger back. He would rather live a life of chastity than risk another fall.

He could imagine June telling her lawyer all about how her husband had failed in his duties in the bedroom and how he'd denied her that pleasure for nearly two decades. His face reddened at the thought. The truth was, all his libido had disappeared a few months after he had recovered from his breakdown, and he'd never even had the slightest urge. It was as if he was denying himself the right to feel any pleasure at all because he had ended a life. Emily Baxter would no longer have the chance to feel anything anymore. She was dead, and he was to blame.

He could not deny that something this central to a relationship gave June the right to end the marriage, and in a strange way he felt relieved. For many years he had lived in the fear that he might be asked to perform when he knew it would be impossible. The thought of it being written as grounds for divorce on a petition that would be read by judges, solicitors, barristers, and others, did make him feel cold, though, and he wished he could make it go away. But wasn't this due punishment? In the old days were not criminals humiliated in public for the crimes they had committed? In medieval times, the stocks were used. Also, he remembered his mother telling him about the village she grew up in, in Cyprus. There, criminals were tied to posts and the rest of the villagers could do whatever they wanted: spit on them, urinate on them, throw things at them. Somehow, he felt he was getting away lightly by just having a petition written about how useless he was in the bedroom.

June asking him to leave and the divorce; these were things he had reaped. He knew he deserved them. In his heart, he felt he'd been given much more in life than he deserved. Ever since the death of Emily Baxter, he'd been waiting for his own world to fall apart; some part of him wanted it to. He wanted punishment.

Often, he asked himself why he didn't just go to the police and solve the unsolved file, close the case, own up. But he never came close to doing that. Why? He didn't know. The most likely reason, which he tried to deny, was that he was a coward as well as a murderer. Somehow, the murder was a secret that must remain in the depths of his soul. He reasoned that the torture he endured each day by holding onto this secret was far more severe than if he were to confess and serve a few years in jail. He didn't want to admit it, get locked up, and then be released. Emily would never have a chance to start her life again, so why should he? By keeping this to himself, he felt, in a twisted way, that he was respecting her memory more by suffering for each day of his existence for what he had done to her and her unborn child. At least that's what he preferred to believe.

After his daughter's phone call, Nigel was left feeling once again like an outsider in his family. He'd felt it when they all lived together, and he felt it again now. He knew the reasons. He'd always kept his distance from them. He was tainted. He didn't want any of that to rub off on them.

Annabelle had ended the phone call by telling him that she would call the estate agents and have them take the house off the market. He had not argued. How could he? This breakup... it was all his fault. Everything was all his fault.

Chapter 17

Nigel walked towards the old house that contained his studio flat, in the former attic of the building. The ground floor and first floor of the building remained empty, untenanted. Almost as if people knew that by renting in that house, they would be sharing their home with a murderer. Nigel knew, though, that the real reason the house was unpopular was because it was at the end of the street, adjacent to a pub and next door to a house rumoured to be a brothel. It was in a dilapidated state of repair. The roof was missing more than a few tiles, and two of the windows in Nigel's flat had cracks that threatened to shatter at any moment. The water pressure was particularly bad on the top floor where Nigel lodged. The water came out in a trickle and was hardly ever warm enough for a shower or bath.

The house was in a run-down area, a hot spot for crime. Many of the houses on the street had boarded up windows and at least two of them had squatters living in them. Nigel wondered why he had not just broken in and squatted in one of the empty houses rather than pay rent for a less-than-habitable flat, but ever since the murder, it was out of the question for Nigel to do anything even slightly against the law; it was as if his conscience forbade him to step over any lines for fear of completely stepping over for good into the life of a criminal. Like alcoholics who avoid even a drop of alcohol in case they slip back into their old obsession. There was also that latent fear of getting caught. If he was arrested for some petty crime and his fingerprints or DNA samples were taken, that might be some way to link him back to the murder of Emily Baxter. He felt like someone living underground, on the run—always having to stay one step ahead of the authorities.

The studio flat had been advertised in the local paper and had been the cheapest flat available. It was, at least, furnished—even if the furniture had seen better days.

As he flopped onto the sofa bed, and tried to tune the ancient portable TV so that he could see the picture rather than a fuzzy screen, he began to worry about how he would keep up the rent payments. His job did not pay well. He'd initially agreed with June that they'd sell the house and split the proceeds. He'd intended to use that money for everyday living expenses, knowing that his wages would only go so far. Now, though, June would be living in the house until house prices picked up, which in the current financial crisis and with current forecasts could be the twelfth of never.

He thought back to when he'd been successful as a young man. He'd worked for a large multinational company in the I.T. department. He'd paid off most of the mortgage within a few years. June had been able to stop working when they'd started a family. How different his life had been then, and how different it could have been now, but in a fit of rage he had wiped all those possibilities away; like taking an eraser to a blackboard, all that was left was the blackness.

The constant regret made him feel seasick. He decided to go to sleep without eating supper. He would have to save what money he had.

Nigel sat staring out of the window in the living area of the flat the next day. It was 1 p.m. When he had first started staring out of the window, it had been 8.30 a.m., he had noticed the rain. He had been getting ready for work, then hearing a rumble of thunder he cursed the weather, thinking: *It's supposed to be summer. We haven't had one day yet where it hasn't rained. It's July, for God's sake!*

As he'd looked at the window, the rain streaming down like tears, for some reason his mind went back to a memory far away. He couldn't put his finger on it but was curious to recall that memory. Moments later, flashes of lightning brought with them flashes of the night he'd killed Emily, and the scene played out before him. He remembered driving home in the pouring rain afterwards. When he pulled his eyes away from the window, he was unaware of the time that had gone by, but knew he felt hungry. *But I've just had breakfast*, he thought, pushing away the feeling of hunger and trying to ignore the sounds his stomach was making. The rain had stopped and the sun had come out. The day was now bright. *That's so strange,* he thought. *A moment ago, it was pouring with rain, now it's sunny.* He shrugged. *British weather!* He shook his head and looked at his watch, sensing he was late for work. *One o'clock? It's stopped*, he thought. Then he looked at the kitchen clock and the carriage clock on the sideboard. His mind raced. He remembered times in the past when he had lost hours from his day, just staring into nothing. That was when he was going through the early stages of his nervous breakdown. Fear gripped him. Could it be happening again?

He switched on the TV, in denial, but he saw the fuzzy picture showing the lunchtime news. It was confirmed. Four hours of his life had passed him by as he stared out of the window. It had only seemed like minutes.

He rushed out of the door, concerned about his state of mind. The word *catatonic* flittered in and out of his consciousness, almost sounding louder than the constant hum of *murderer, murderer, murderer...*

Passing a homeless man wrapped in a sleeping bag, a dog lying beside him, Nigel had an uncomfortable thought: this could be him in a couple of months if he wasn't careful. If he lost his job now, he'd have no way of supporting himself and there was a recession on. Jobs were few and far between.

Luckily for him, nobody had noticed his absence from work that morning; one of the advantages of working for a large company where people were anonymous. Also, it helped that he worked in an office on his own in a part of the building that was not commonly used. He found a few messages on his computer about things he had to do, but as far as he could tell, no one had tried to contact him; or if they had, they'd probably assumed he had just popped out of the room.

Nigel hadn't eaten anything since breakfast and the hunger pangs started up again. He left the building and headed up the high street to get a sandwich. As he paid for his lunch, he realised that he would have to start thinking of ways to cut the cost of living. He resented paying three pounds for a sandwich when he could make one himself for half the price; all he needed was a cheap loaf of bread each week and a few bits and pieces for fillings.

Stepping out of the café, the glare of the sun made him squint. He decided that, as it had turned out to be a warm day, he would take the opportunity to get some fresh air and eat his lunch in the park. When he walked through the gates and saw the first bench, he noticed that it looked damp from the rain that had fallen earlier. He sighed, but determined not to be defeated, he looked around and saw a newspaper that someone had discarded flapping in the wind not far from the bench. He laid it on the bench and sat on top of it. He reminisced over how, years ago, he used to buy the *Evening Standard* each day, but now, it was given away free; and more often than not, he would find copies of it strewn along the pavements of the city as he walked home from work.

He sat down and took the wrapping off his sandwich. Leaning back on the bench as he ate, he watched people in the park. There were a few young boys, maybe ten years old, kicking a ball around on the grass, and there were a handful of people on lunch breaks eating their sandwiches as they walked along the path through the park, but somehow the place appeared derelict, bereft of life.

Nigel took a bite of his sandwich, then he heard a voice.

'Hello, sorry I've forgotten your name.' The young girl sat next to him. 'Do you mind if I join you?' she asked in a voice that sounded familiar, yet Nigel could not place it. The sun was in his eyes. He tried to chew the rather large mouthful he had taken, as quickly as he could, so that he would be able to respond to her. He had not looked at her yet, for fear of her seeing crumbs exploding from his mouth. As quickly as he could manage, he finished the bite of food and turned towards her. He could only stare when he laid eyes on her. It was Kelly, from work. The Emily Baxter look-alike. A panic surged through him. *What does she want from me?*

'Oh, this bench is a bit wet,' she said, standing up and taking her sandwich out of the plastic carrier bag she was holding. She laid the bag on the bench. 'That's better.'

She smiled and he tried to regain his composure, telling himself that he was overreacting. It was just a coincidence that she looked so much like Emily... But there was something nagging him that would not go away. It was at the back of his mind and he was purposefully avoiding thinking about it, fearful that if he listened to the nagging voice, somehow, his world would fall apart.

'Sorry, you probably don't remember me,' she continued, 'I'm Kelly, we met a couple of days ago... in the office...'

'Ye... Yes, I remember you,' he said, looking down at his sandwich, her brown eyes burning themselves into his mind, memories of Emily's eyes haunted his vision. He didn't feel hungry now. He held the sandwich as it became increasingly soggy, wanting to throw it away, but then thinking of how much he had paid for it.

'I hope you won't take this the wrong way,' said the girl, 'but you remind me of my grandfather.'

Nigel laughed nervously. 'Oh,' he said, feeling suddenly old. He knew he was definitely old enough to be her father at least, and he knew that he had let himself go and looked older than his 55 years, but somehow the comment still stung.

There was silence as Kelly stared ahead of her. Nigel took another bite of his sandwich, hoping to somehow find the appetite to finish it.

Kelly took the plastic wrapper off her sandwich and began to eat. He noticed she had placed a red leather handbag on the bench beside her. It was small, with a fabric rose design on one side. The bag looked familiar, and he briefly wondered whether maybe June had owned a similar one; but then his eyes widened as he remembered where he had seen a bag like that before. It was Emily's bag... he'd gone to such lengths to get rid of it. He shook his head slowly.

'Are you okay?' she asked, snapping him out of his dark thoughts.

'Um... yes, fine.'

Kelly followed his eyes and looked at her bag briefly, then smiled at him. He pulled his eyes away from the bag and tried to concentrate on his sandwich, pushing away all other thoughts.

'I suppose we'll be seeing a lot of each other,' she said. 'There's always so much photocopying to be done in my department.'

Curiosity got the better of Nigel as he remembered the confusion the other day when he had first met her: 'Er... what department do you work in?' Flashes of the newspaper articles she had asked him to copy momentarily filled his mind.

'Forensics,' she said, wiping her mouth with her hand to remove a crumb.

'Oh, I didn't know there was a forensics department.' This made Nigel realise just how cut off he was from the rest of the legal firm in his isolated office in the basement.

'Yes,' said Kelly, interrupting his thoughts, 'there is a forensics department. We deal with quite a lot of crime. Some is routine, but there's also the gory stuff, like murder. The team often visits murder scenes, and they come back with lots of stories.'

Murderer... murderer... murderer. The words increased their pace and ferocity in Nigel's head. He bit into his sandwich.

'I'm three months pregnant,' said Kelly, unexpectedly.

Nigel's mouth became dry and he feared he would choke on the bite of food he'd just taken.

'That's so refreshing!' said Kelly, brightly, turning towards him. She smiled, and he noticed pieces of salad and sauce from her sandwich in between her perfect straight white teeth. 'You're cool! Most people always say "congratulations" when I tell them I'm pregnant. It's so fake. Most times, I know that the women are jealous or thinking I'm a tart because I'm not in a relationship, and the men just congratulate me because they think that's what I want to hear. You're different. You're like my granddad; he never hides his true feelings, always says what's on his mind. He told me life's too short to play games. Thank you for not congratulating me!'

Nigel did not really know what to say. He was still pondering what she'd said about never hiding his true feelings... he was *always* hiding his true feelings... How could he not? How ironic that Kelly had thought he wasn't a *fake*.

Kelly chewed the last bite of her sandwich and threw the wrapping in the bin beside the bench. When she returned to her seat she turned towards him. Her eyes lost their sparkle as she said, 'I don't know who the father is.'

Nigel did not know where to look. Why was she confiding in him? He tried avoiding her eyes by looking straight ahead. The young boys who had been playing football were now looking in his direction. One of them was pointing at him, he noticed, and another two were laughing.

Perhaps they think I'm Kelly's boyfriend? he thought, and brushed it off.

'I've been living with a bloke for years, but I found out he's into all sorts of criminal activity. I've been seeing Ramiro for a few months. He's such a good guy. I'm hoping the child is his. I've been planning to leave Russ, my old boyfriend, for ages.'

Russ? Ramiro? Those were the names of Emily Baxter's boyfriends. How? Who was this Kelly? She said she worked in forensics. Suddenly, a thought struck him like a thunderbolt: *What if they know I killed Emily? They might have evidence. They might be trying to entrap me... get some information... a confession.*

Why would a young girl come and spill her secrets to a complete stranger? Nigel became wary. He would have to keep his lips sealed; try to say as little as possible.

The boys in the park had gone back to kicking their ball around.

'Sorry to burden you with my problems,' said Kelly. 'You just seem like such a nice man. I know it sounds stupid, as we've only just met, but I feel I can trust you. Do you have children?'

The guilt rose again from the pit of Nigel's stomach at the question that always made him nervous. Yes, he did have children, but Emily Baxter didn't get the chance. 'Um, yes, I have two,' he said, staring at his hands.

'That's nice,' said Kelly. 'Two is a nice number. I've always loved children, and I always said I wanted five. It just seems like the perfect amount. I wanted three girls and two boys, and I've already decided on their names...' She paused.

Nigel dared to look up at her with a sideways glance and spotted what he thought were tears threatening to fall.

She sighed and looked at him, shrugging. 'But things don't always turn out as we plan, do they?' The sadness in her eyes made him queasy. Her eyes were so similar to Emily's.

'You're young,' said Nigel tearing his eyes away from that dark stare and trying to lighten the mood. 'You can still have those five children.'

Kelly laughed. 'Yes, maybe.' Then she held onto her stomach. 'The sad thing is, I don't know whether I want to keep this one. Abortion is like murder, though, isn't it? I don't think I could live with myself if...' Her voice faded away and the voices in Nigel's head began to boom louder so that the air around him was filled with their resonating pulse: *Murderer, murderer, murderer...* The chant raged at the forefront of his mind as though Kelly's words had set off some kind of explosion. He tried to think of other things to drown out the accusatory words.

'Do your children still live at home?' asked Kelly.

'Er... no.' Nigel fought the words that were battling in his head and threatening to find their way out via his tongue. 'My son is at university, and my daughter lives with her partner.' He felt relieved to get to the end of the sentence.

'I went to university,' said Kelly with a wistful look and a sigh, as if talking about a long-lost dream. 'I did physics. I fancied a boy who was doing science and hoped if I knew what it all meant, then I could impress him. It didn't work, of course. I ended up dropping out after the first year. Then I met Russ. We moved in together. He was so nice at first, really fooled me.'

Nigel was hardly concentrating on what Kelly was saying. All he could think about was that Emily Baxter had been to university to study physics; he'd read about it in a newspaper.

Nigel began to worry that this girl sitting next to him might be the ghost of Emily Baxter. Had she come back to haunt him? There were just too many coincidences. But she didn't look like a ghost, she looked real... but then again, what does a ghost look like? He'd never seen a ghost. He began to feel haunted.

Kelly looked at her watch. 'Oh, well, must dash. It was nice to see you again, Nigel.'

'And you,' he said as she walked away. His mind was in disarray. She'd called him by his name, but when she'd first sat down, she said she'd forgotten it. Nothing made sense.

One of the young boys shouted across to him, 'Losing your marbles, Granddad?' The other boys laughed.

Nigel felt threatened and stood up to leave. He bowed his head as he walked towards the park gates, feeling bemused.

Later that afternoon, Nigel was in his office when Abigail Johnson entered. She was one of the administrators from the litigation department. Nigel often chatted with Abigail. Well, she was the one who talked. She was very chatty and always had a lot to say whenever she was delivering the mail.

'Hi Nige!' she said cheerily. 'How's it going?'

He watched as she placed a pile of envelopes into the sorting box.

'Oh, mustn't grumble,' he replied.

'That bad, hey?' Abigail pushed her glasses back up her nose, as they'd slipped slightly. She continued, 'Nige, how long have you worked here?'

'About sixteen years, give or take.'

'That's a hell of a long time. Don't you think you've paid your dues? Have you thought of moving on, doing something else? The longest I've ever stayed in a job is four years, and I was itching to get out. It must get pretty mundane here. You should spread your wings a bit.'

'I'm a bit old to start thinking of changing jobs.'

'Old? You're not old. How old are you? If you don't mind me asking.'

'Fifty-five.'

'That's young. Didn't you tell me once that you used to work in I.T.? Why not do that? Computers are the way forward. People can't live without them. I heard that Colin from I.T. might be leaving. He's thinking of retiring. Maybe you could get his job?' Abigail twisted a ringlet of blonde hair around her fingers as she spoke. 'If you ask me, it's about time he left. He's no bloody good, anyway. Every time he fixes something, another thing goes wrong.' She rolled her eyes.

Nigel frowned and looked at his hands. 'I.T. has changed a lot since I was a specialist.'

'Yeah, well, it's changed a lot since Colin was a young man... How old must he be now? About seventy? I don't think computers were even invented in his day. If you ask me, they need someone like you, Nige. Remember you told me how to fix my computer screen when it was blank that day and I came to ask you because Colin wasn't around?'

'Er... was that the day you realised it wasn't plugged in?'

Abigail blushed slightly. 'Well, I am blonde. I suppose I have a reputation to live up to.' She laughed and said, 'Anyway, I think

137

you should go for his job when he leaves. It'll all come back to you when you start working again; it'll be like riding a bike. You'll soon get back into the swing of things. Computers can't have changed that much since you were a specialist.'

He smiled sadly, then tried to put on a cheerful face.

'Nige?' She walked closer to him as if she were about to reveal a secret, and sat on the stool next to his desk. 'You've been working here much longer than me. You must know a lot about the people here. Do you know anything about a bloke called Ken in the criminal litigation department? Tall, black hair, blue eyes.'

'Ken Braithwaite?'

'I don't know his surname. I've only met him once. Our departments don't have much to do with each other, and being a criminal lawyer, he's out and about so much, hardly ever in. We met at one of the staff get-togethers last week and he gave me his telephone number. He was quite flirty, but he had been drinking. Do you know him?'

'I've only met him at Christmas parties and other such things,' said Nigel. 'I've only spoken to him a couple of times. I think he's worked here about ten years or so.'

'I was going to ask your opinion of him. He seems nice, but you never know, do you? For all I know, he could be the office letch.'

Nigel put on a laugh. 'I haven't heard anything like that about him. Why don't you go out with him and see what you think?'

'Yes, I think I might do that.' She smiled and stood up. 'Thanks for helping me make up my mind.'

'It's surprising how little I know about this company considering I've been here so long,' he pondered out loud. He'd been reminded of his chat with Kelly at the park. 'Do you know, I didn't even realise we have a forensics department.'

'We have a forensics department?' Abigail raise her eyebrows. 'I didn't know that, either.'

'Yes, I met Kelly from Forensics the other day for the first time. I suppose it's quite a large company; two people can be working here for ages and never meet.'

'Yes, like me and Ken.' Abigail's eyes had a sparkle that showed her mind had gone off into some kind of dream for a few seconds.

She walked towards the door. 'I've taken up enough of your time, Nige. It was nice to chat.' She stuck her head through the gap in the door, before she left, and smiled. 'I'll be back to report what happens with me and Ken; I'll fill you in on all the juicy gossip.'

Chapter 18

The next morning, just as Nigel was about to leave for work, an envelope fell through the letterbox and onto his shoes. It was a brown envelope franked with the name of the local county court. He knew what it was before he opened it. June had been to see a solicitor and he was expecting to receive the divorce petition. 'As soon as you get it, can you sign it and send it back to the court,' Annabelle had said, during their last telephone conversation, 'We have to get the divorce finalised quickly; Mum's not taking this well.'

What about how I'm feeling? the thought flitted through his mind but was then quickly replaced by the next thought, the ever-present reminder: *Murderer...* and the familiar feeling of unworthiness, the feeling that he deserved to be punished for ever more. Flashes of that night so long ago remained embedded in his mind and flickered on and off like an old movie, catching him when he least expected it.

He opened the envelope. The letter told him he could seek legal advice before signing the form if he so wished, but what was the point? He fished out the form he needed to sign, and the reply-paid envelope. He ticked the box to state he was not contesting the divorce, and took the envelope with him as he exited the flat.

It struck him that this day had been coming for twenty years—since the day he hit Emily Baxter with the hammer. The fuse had been lit on the wire that burned away, year after year. Now, the flame had reached its end. He thought back to the early years when he had first met June and the good times they had shared, but he knew he had destroyed that. His anger, his inability to control his temper, to keep it at bay, meant that he was here now, alone.

He felt a sadness in his heart when he realised that June had really loved him once. He knew that he, too, had loved her, but he could hardly remember what that felt like. Ever since the killing he had considered himself unworthy of love, slowly but surely distancing himself from anyone who showed him that emotion. He built his wall, denying himself that which Emily Baxter would never be able to feel again... because of him.

He slipped the envelope into the post box and walked on.

As he walked towards his office building, he noticed Abigail was chatting with Ken outside. She was obviously flirting with him, twiddling her hair between her fingers and staring up into his eyes whilst fluttering her eyelashes. Ken leaned forward and kissed her cheek. She blushed and waved to him as she walked into the building. So, she had taken his advice and decided to go out with Ken, he mused. At the same time, Nigel heard some shouting, but could not be sure where it was coming from.

'I never want to see you again, you slut! You've been cheating on me. How do you even know the baby is mine?' a man's angry voice boomed.

'It's definitely yours, Russ!' came a high-pitched scream, which he recognised as Kelly's voice. Yet he could still not really make out where the voices were coming from.

'You're saying that so that I won't kill you, aren't you, bitch?'

'No... no... please believe me...'

Nigel heard crying. He looked around to see where Kelly was but couldn't see her. Shaking his head, he walked into the building. As he got into the lift, Kelly walked in behind him, wiping her eyes with a tissue.

The doors closed behind them. Now they were alone.

'Er... are you okay?' asked Nigel.

'Sorry. You probably heard that row with my boyfriend. He was walking me to work, but then he started going on about something he'd heard in the pub, about one of his friends seeing me kissing another man. He's taken my keys and thrown me out on the streets even though I'm expecting a baby. Okay, it might not be his, but it might be...' She was getting more and more worked up as she spoke, her cheeks blazing.

'He's probably just angry.' Nigel closed his eyes when he said that. Sighing, he continued: 'He wouldn't throw you out when you're pregnant.'

'He doesn't believe the baby is his. I have nowhere to go. I'm homeless and pregnant. You have to help me.' Her eyes were full of unshed tears as she pleaded. He was reminded again of that night when the rain had been falling; Emily's eyes had had the same lost look in them.

Nigel looked at the floor embarrassed, not sure what to say. The lift doors opened at the fourth floor, where the canteen was situated. Nigel had been meaning to get a cup of coffee for himself before going to his office. 'A cup of tea or coffee might make you feel better,' he said as he stepped out of the lift.

'I don't want a cup of tea or coffee,' she replied morosely. 'Is there any way I could stay with you until this blows over? I won't be any bother. You'll hardly know I'm there.' She touched her stomach and looked up at him with those eyes that looked like wells.

'I only have a studio flat. It's very small.'

'That's okay, I don't have much stuff, and it would really only be a place for me to sleep at night. I won't be around much, I promise. Please?'

Nigel wondered whether this was some kind of karmic payback. He would be forced to live with a woman who looked so similar to the woman he had killed. But how could he turn her away? She was pregnant.

'What about your parents? Can't you stay with them?'

'No. They... We don't get on.'

'You mentioned your grandfather the other day; you said I reminded you of him... what about...'

'He died last year.'

'Oh, I'm sorry... Well... what about your other boyfriend—'

'Ramiro? Oh, he was nothing special... just a fling. I just needed someone to distract me from my miserable life with Russ. If I move in with Ramiro, he'll get the wrong idea. I'd be leading him on. No. It's just me and my baby. We're all alone in the world. We need your help, Nigel. Will you help us?'

Will you help us? Nigel was hooked by this plea... *Perhaps, if I help her, I could... in some way, make up for... what I did to* her... *to Em... that girl. Okay... no... nothing would make up for that, but... but I could do something* good, *for once.*

'Okay. You can stay tonight and we'll see how it works out,' he said.

The relief was clear on her face. 'You're a lifesaver, Nigel. You really are such a good friend. Thank you. Let's meet up in the park at lunchtime and we'll talk about it.' She smiled as she walked away.

Just then, Philip, who worked in the HR department, walked past him and said, 'I always think people are talking to themselves when they have those mobiles with earplugs... gets me every time.' He laughed as he walked towards the canteen.

At first, Nigel was confused as to why he'd said that, but then he realised that he still had his earplugs in his ears, from when he'd been listening to his iPod on his way in to work. He pulled them out and walked to the canteen. As he poured himself a cup of coffee, he wondered how he would explain to his children that he had a young girl living with him *and* that she was pregnant.

Then, he felt sad as he realised that he didn't have much contact with his children, anyway, so it was hardly likely they'd find out about Kelly. His children didn't seem too concerned about what he did. They hadn't been to visit him since he'd moved to London. He'd had precisely two phone calls from his daughter and those had been about the divorce and about letting June stay at the house. His son had disappeared into university life. He hadn't heard anything from him at all. He could hardly blame them, though, as he had never really taken much of an interest in their lives as they were growing up. Another legacy from the one day he'd regret for the rest of his life. It had impacted on so much of his future. Perhaps his relationship with his children would have been perfect if he had not been a murderer... He could only guess at that.

***

At lunchtime, Nigel left his office with a feeling of trepidation. His paranoia had escalated ever since he had first met Kelly. There were just too many things about her that reminded him of Emily. Was she a detective? Had the case been reopened, and was Kelly a plant to try to get him to reveal information to pin the murder on him? Is that the reason June had left him? Did she know? Had she known all these years and kept her mouth shut for the sake of the children? Had she seen him in his bloody clothes that night? Perhaps she had woken up to go to the toilet, or heard some noise downstairs that had woken her. All she would have had to have done was lean over the banister and she would have seen him frantically using the kitchen scissors to shred his clothes. If she had seen him, perhaps she had put two and two together when she saw the news about Emily's death months later, when the story had appeared on *Crimewatch*. She wouldn't have wanted to believe it—was probably in denial for a while... her husband... Nigel... a murderer? If she had thought about it, she would have probably been able to believe it, though. He'd always been loud, aggressive, spoke his mind, often walking over other people's feelings in the process. And she had hated his taste in music. He liked heavy metal. She had always told him that it was violent music. She always said he drove faster and became angry more easily in the car when he was listening to that music. He always retorted that the reason he was angry in the car was because she was with him. But she wasn't with him when he'd murdered Emily.

As much as he would love to have something to blame his rage on, he knew it wasn't June and it wasn't the music... it was a part of him... something inside him that had caused him to react in the way he had that night. That was why he tried so hard ever since to keep himself under control.

As he contemplated all of this, he began to imagine that if June had seen him cutting up his clothes that night, she may well have looked in the bin later and maybe even kept some of the clothes as evidence. She wouldn't have wanted to tell the police while the children were still growing up; how could she let them grow up knowing that their own father was a murderer? Good old June, she'd bided her time, waited until they were independent, and now she had gone to the police, taking her evidence. Perhaps they were now setting him up. Kelly would be getting to know him... gaining his trust... moving in with him! That would make it easier for her to search his belongings. *That's ridiculous.* He shook his head. If it was the police, they would hardly have Kelly pretend to be in a similar position to Emily; they wouldn't want to give the game away. But maybe it was a tactic, to force him to breaking point as the memories flooded back to haunt him.

No, no! Kelly is just a girl who needs my help.

His other theory bordered on lunacy, but he couldn't ignore the thoughts that continually entered his mind. He was becoming more convinced that Kelly was really Emily's ghost come back to haunt him and leave him with a constant reminder of what he had done to her. But then he realised he didn't need a constant physical reminder of what he'd done... it was there in his head, and had never gone away. It lived and breathed with him. He could never forget.

He had been sitting on the park bench for about five minutes when she arrived.

'Nigel!' Kelly sat next to him. She was smiling brightly.

'Kelly, hello.' He forced a smile back.

'Thanks for meeting me here. And thanks for letting me stay with you at your place. It's such a weight off my mind.' She frowned slightly, and continued, 'I promise you it won't be for long. Only until I find somewhere else.'

Nigel nodded and took his homemade sandwiches out of his bag. He saw that Kelly didn't have any lunch with her. 'Er... would you like a sandwich? I made them myself. Egg and tomato.'

'I'm not very hungry,' she replied. 'But thanks for offering.'

He bit into his sandwich. When he had swallowed, he turned to Kelly and said, 'I can help you find somewhere else to rent. It didn't take me long to find my flat when I moved here.' He thought of his flat in the deserted building. He began to worry that Kelly might get the idea of renting one of the empty flats below his, and then he would have to see her every day. He felt an urgency to try to find her somewhere else to live. 'We'll go to the estate agents together tomorrow, okay?'

An elderly woman frowned at Nigel as she walked past the bench. When he caught her eye, she looked away quickly, almost wary of him. Nigel looked beyond the old woman and noticed the same group of young boys that had played in the park when he'd last been there with Kelly. The boy who had made fun of him the last time was looking his way and laughing.

Nigel began to feel self-conscious. It was odd that people looked at him in such a way whenever he was with Kelly. Granted, he was older than her, but many older men dated younger women. Even if they assumed he was dating her, why was it so ridiculous in their eyes? *Do I look* that *old?*

He knew the years had not been kind to him. When he looked in a mirror, he could not deny that he would easily pass for someone in his late sixties. At a funeral the year before, June's father, aged 80, had looked younger than him.

The truth was that he had hardly paid attention to his appearance since 1991. That had just not been a priority.

As he pondered this, he was left baffled because he knew he looked old enough to be Kelly's father, so why were people looking at him in such a strange way when they saw him with her? He never kissed her or held her hand. He'd never even hugged her, so why did they assume he was somehow romantically linked to her? Why did people assume they were a couple and not a father and daughter out having lunch together... or even just friends? Maybe it was because she was pregnant and people automatically assume the person she's with must be the father.

Then, he began to question his mind. Maybe he was just imagining that the people were looking at him; maybe he was too paranoid—a by-product of all the years he had waited for that knock on the door and for the police to be standing there, for justice to be served. Or, perhaps people looked at him that way because of his scruffy, unkempt appearance, not only because he was with Kelly. Perhaps the time had come for him to start putting some effort into making himself more presentable.

Kelly had not said much since the old woman walked past, and when Nigel turned towards her he saw that she was crying. Not audibly. A tear was drifting down her cheek and another fell from her chin. She made no effort to wipe them away.

'Kelly? Are you all right?' he asked.

She sniffed and wiped her tears with her sleeve. 'Yes, yes, I'm fine. I just feel all alone in the world. I'm feeling sorry for myself, that's all. Ignore me.' The bright smile was pulled out of its box again and Nigel realised that even though she wore it often and it looked real, it covered up a great deal of pain. He recognised the trick. He'd used it himself, many times.

Something in her eyes was reaching out to him as she said, 'Can I stay with you until I have my baby? I... I'm scared to go through it alone.'

Nigel froze. It was as if he found himself back there: back in August 1991, on the night that had stolen his future, looking into Emily Baxter's eyes. The same look Emily had worn, emanated from Kelly's deep brown stare; one of fear, one of desperation. Her eyes were so much like Emily's that he was starting to feel that through getting to know Kelly, he was learning a bit more

147

about the girl whose life he'd cut short; Emily's eyes had been hiding pain, too.

'There's not much room in my flat.'

A football landed under the bench, and two boys ran towards it.

'Sorry, Granddad,' said one of the boys. He wore a hooded top, even though the sun had come out and it had turned into a warm day.

The other boy, who wore white shorts, a bright red T-shirt, and a baseball cap, leaned under the bench and took the ball. 'Sorry to interrupt your chat,' he said.

The other boy laughed and made a gesture with his hands, clapping his fingers onto his thumb to imitate a mouth opening and closing.

The two boys laughed until they had to hold their stomachs and then ran towards the rest of the group.

'Children, these days, have no respect for older people,' said Nigel. 'In fact, I doubt they would know how to hold a conversation, they spend so much time on the Internet and playing computer games.'

'I agree with you, Nigel. I sat next to a couple of teenagers in *McDonald's* recently, and they didn't say a word to each other. One of them was texting on his phone the whole time, or maybe checking his Facebook page. The art of conversation is dying.'

Nigel finished his sandwich in silence and then gave Kelly his address. She wrote it down on a piece of newspaper she found on the ground.

'I'll eat out tonight, I don't want to get in your way,' she said as she stood up to leave. 'I'll get to your place at about nine, so you can show me where I'm to sleep.'

'Okay, that's fine,' he said. He watched her exit the park.

As he walked back to his office that afternoon, he felt nervous. He didn't want Kelly to move in with him. He'd hardly spoken to June for twenty years, but they had a big house; he had avoided her by going into different rooms. The flat was so small, he would be forced to interact with Kelly. He recalled what she'd said about the "art of conversation dying"; he was not much of a conversationalist, at least not since the murder. It was all he could do, most days, to stop the overflow of toxic, accusatory voices spilling out of his mouth, as the chant of *Murderer... murderer... murderer*, played as constant background music. The less he spoke, the less chance there was of him saying something that could link him to the death.

It was going to be difficult to avoid Kelly in such a small place. There was only one room, unless he wanted to hide in the shower or toilet. On top of all that, she reminded him so much of Emily and of the thing he had been trying to forget for over a third of his existence.

Chapter 19

For the next few weeks, Nigel had a house guest. He avoided her as much as possible, leaving early for work and eating out in the café, rather than facing Kelly at home. He didn't like talking to her. There was something that kept nagging him; a paranoid feeling that she was not who she said she was. Some days he was utterly convinced she was Emily Baxter back from the dead to wreak revenge.

One evening, about a week into her stay, he walked into the flat at about 9.20 p.m. and found her on the sofa bed in the living area. She was sitting up, watching his TV. As if she had been waiting for him to return, as soon as he closed the door, she began to speak: 'Nigel, there's something I haven't told you.'

He wondered whether it would be easier to leave the flat now, keep walking and never return, so that he would not have to hear what she had to say. Was this going to be the moment when she revealed that she was an undercover police officer and that she would now be arresting him on suspicion of murder? He had anticipated this moment for so long. He was so sure he would be found out. Every person he met was a potential undercover cop. He had never felt fully at ease with anyone since that evening in 1991.

'Hi Kelly... um... I'll just make a cup of tea and then we can talk.' He walked over to the kitchen area. Whatever she wanted to tell him, he wanted to put it off for as long as possible.

'Okay,' she said and continued to stare at the TV screen in front of her.

When Nigel had finished preparing his tea, he pulled a chair next to the sofa bed where Kelly was seated. He sat down, feeling jittery, as if he were about to be told the results of a very important surgical procedure. His heart beat loudly against his chest.

As he raised his eyes, he noticed the television screen and could see the fuzzy picture was showing this week's *Crimewatch*.

"Our next case concerns some missing jewellery, stolen from a renowned jewellers in central London." The presenter wore a frown as he spoke.

Nigel imagined June seated in front of the television right now watching this programme. Somewhere inside him, a yearning to return to the life he used to know reared its head, but he knew that he could never go back. Melancholia took hold. He'd had so much to be grateful for before he threw it all away in a fit of rage. *June used to love me. Once.*

'Nigel,' began Kelly. 'How was work?'

'Not bad,' he muttered almost incoherently. 'Um... did you mention you had something to tell me?' He felt a need to hear it now. He'd mentally prepared himself for the worst as he'd stirred his tea, and didn't want to be kept waiting in case his resolve lost its tight grip.

'Yes. It's no coincidence that you and I are living together. I have been searching for you for some time. Years, in fact.'

Nigel's eyes widened.

'Wh... Why?' was all he could say.

'Are you saying you don't remember me?'

'I... I....' The only image in his mind was of the dead girl. Emily. But that didn't make sense. Had she somehow survived? But the police had found a body... was that a different girl? *No... this girl, Kelly, is too young.*

'My real name is Emily. Kelly is just a name I picked because I didn't want to spook you when we first met.'

Nigel stood up. His face was pale.

'Sit down, Nigel. I know this must have come as a shock. I'm Emily Baxter.' Those dark eyes bore through him and he felt himself shake involuntarily.

He walked towards the front door. 'This is some sort of dream... nightmare... You're a figment of my imagination... You're not real.' Beads of sweat formed on his forehead.

'Oh, I'm real, Nigel. I'm Emily Baxter. The woman you killed.'

'No!' screamed Nigel. He felt his head pounding, the blood surging frantically. This could not be happening. The very next moment, he found himself stirring his tea, standing by the kitchen bench, and when he turned around towards the living area, Kelly was sitting on the sofa bed staring at the TV, as she had been when he first walked in. She smiled at him when he looked at her.

Hesitantly, with the feeling that he was stuck in some sort of dream that kept repeating itself, he walked towards the sofa. What would happen now? Had he really imagined what just occurred, or had it actually happened? His recollection blurred.

He pulled the chair towards the sofa with a feeling of déjà vu, and sat down. He looked at the TV screen. *Crimewatch.*

"Our next case concerns some missing jewellery, stolen from a renowned jewellers in central London."

Nigel didn't know if he should sigh with relief. It seemed he had only imagined his conversation with Kelly, but he was shocked at how vivid and real it had been. Was it a portent? Some sort of premonition? Should he make his escape now before she began to speak? Would he end up living the rest of his days in this room in a lost segment of time that replayed for eternity? *Have I lost my mind?*

'Hi,' said Kelly, 'Good day at work?'

'Um...' He shook in fear of what she would say next. Steadying the swaying cup in his hands, he looked at the TV. 'It was quiet,' he mumbled.

'I have something to tell you. Something I should have told you before, but...' She paused.

He dared to turn towards her and saw her eyes were wet. A tear fell down one of her cheeks and she didn't try to wipe it away, as if she hadn't noticed it, or perhaps tears were so commonplace to her that she did not feel the need. Her eyes stared ahead. She appeared to be deep in thought, or maybe in a trance.

Nigel's heart rate quickened, not for the first time that evening. Panic began to set in. He looked towards the door. An escape route. He wanted to get up and run towards it, leave everything behind, and just keep running.

'It's something I haven't told anyone else, but I feel I can trust you.' Her hands reached up to her face and she wiped away a few stray tears. Her stubborn, fake smile resumed its residency on her face, to disguise her other feelings.

Nigel held his breath.

'I had an abortion last year, and I was thinking of aborting this baby too, but I felt so terrible about the last one. Do you know, when it was the last baby's due date, I cried for three hours non-stop? I thought I would die. I was having trouble breathing by the end of it. Eventually, I blacked out, I think. Then, this year when the abortion date came around, it was like I went into mourning all over again. I felt like I'd killed someone, you know? That baby had died because of me. But still, and I hate myself for it, I was thinking of having another abortion. It just would make more sense. The last baby was Russ's. I'd just found out that he was a drug dealer and that he was part of a gang, so I was going to leave him. I didn't want to have his baby. You know, I spent weeks praying it would just die so I wouldn't have to have it. But after the abortion I felt like a murderer. Just to think, that baby would have been a year old this year. Do you think I'm a bad person, Nigel?'

She looked into his eyes; hers were pleading for some sort of assurance. He could not bear to look at her as the memories surged to his brain.

'I don't think you're bad. You did what you thought was best at the time,' he said, in a quiet voice, staring at his hands. *But I can't say that about what I did*, he thought, darkly.

In the background, *Crimewatch* was showing a reconstruction of a burglary. Nigel and Kelly looked ahead at the screen—a distraction.

After a few minutes, Nigel turned towards Kelly and noticed she was crying again. He handed her a tissue from the box on the sideboard.

'Thanks,' she said. Then her stare met his eyes again: 'It really felt like I'd killed someone. You have no idea how that feels.' She wiped her eyes, blew her nose, and took a few more tissues from the box.

Nigel looked away from her.

'Do you think I should get rid of this baby?' she asked.

Nigel suddenly had a thought: What if Emily Baxter had been planning to abort her baby? Maybe she was wishing it would die, just like Kelly had been with her first child? If so, maybe he could stop feeling so bad about the fact that she was pregnant when he killed her. But all the while, his thoughts confirmed what he knew was true, *Murderer, murderer, murderer...* Wasn't it worse, in fact, that he was now trying to find reasons not to feel guilty for taking a life? Didn't that make him even more cold-blooded?

'No,' he heard himself say, 'don't do it. Life is sacred. You would regret it for ever. It will stay in your mind and you'll never be free. You'll be fighting with your conscience all your life. It will follow you everywhere, you'll never have any peace, there's no escape from it. Your mind will never let you forget that you're a murd...' He stopped himself. *What am I saying? Why did I say that? What else did I say? Did I tell her about Emily?* A cold sweat took hold. *I'm losing it.*

'You talk about it like someone who knows, Nigel... How did you get so wise?'

He crossed his arms in front of him and shook. 'I'm not wise. I... I've just heard people talk about it. By the time a person gets to my age, he's heard a lot of things. Lived through a lot.'

Kelly rubbed her hands together as if trying to warm them up. 'My mum would kill me if she knew I'd had an abortion.'

'Kelly, stop beating yourself up about it. One thing I do know is that we can never go back and change things. We have to live with the consequences of what we've done. There's no point going over it and over it when you can't change things. We have to try to let go or our lives will be stuck. We won't be able to move on. Our whole lives will be lived in a moment of time that we want to change, but we can't do that. It's futile.' Nigel rocked back and forth on his chair as he spoke, tears welling in his eyes.

'So, you think I should keep this baby?'

Nigel sat still and looked at Kelly. He felt paranoid, as if he may have revealed a bit too much to her, but she was looking at him as if awaiting a response.

'Nigel? What do you think? I'll be a single mother. I have no job.'

'But you're working at Bainsworthy.'

'No, I'm not. That was just a temporary contract, and when they found out I was pregnant, they didn't renew it... surprise, surprise.'

'That's illegal. You could take them to a tribunal.'

'Could I?'

'Yes.'

'Could you help me to do that?'

'I'm not a lawyer, but I could help you find one who can take on the case.'

'I was going to tell you sooner about losing my job, but I thought you'd throw me out... I mean, I can't help with the rent here now.'

'Um... I'm sure the local council would be able to find you a flat.'

'Okay, I'll go and see someone at the council.'

They both turned towards the television where the presenter was saying, *"Emily Baxter was found on a remote beach by a passer-by. She appeared to have been hit over the head with a blunt instrument, perhaps a hammer. The killer has never been found. The decision has been made to reopen the case after a request from Emily's sisters. With the advances in DNA testing, the police are hoping that some progress can be made towards finding who is responsible for this crime."*

There followed a reconstruction where an actress with bright red hair depicted Emily arguing with a man who, Nigel saw, looked very similar to him as a young man.

The presenter read out a telephone number that also appeared at the bottom of the TV screen, asking viewers to call in if they could remember anything. Then a computer generated image was put up on the screen as to what the suspect might look like now, based on witness descriptions.

'Wow! That looks like you, Nigel!' said Kelly, laughing. 'Are you the murderer?'

Nigel could only stare ahead at the image on the screen in bewilderment.

'And, she's got bright red hair, like me! Oh my God! It could be me and you.' Kelly's laugh sounded strange in the room that had never known laughter—at least not since Nigel had lived there. The laugh had an almost eerie quality that resounded, like an echo, in Nigel's head; taunting him.

Murderer... murderer... murderer...

The case was being reopened. As Nigel took in the information, it felt like a clock began to tick in his head... Soon, there would be nowhere to hide.

Two weeks later, Kelly moved out. She'd found a new boyfriend, she said. No more mention was made on the news about the Emily Baxter case. Nigel obsessively searched the newspapers and scanned the Internet daily. The only bit of news he could find was that the case was to be reopened. Nigel dared to think that perhaps it would all blow over.

The weeks he'd spent with Kelly as his lodger had been surreal, and he began to doubt any of it had happened. She had hardly been there, anyway. She'd leave the flat before he awoke and return late at night, after midnight. She'd say she'd been clubbing whenever he asked her about it. He caught her in the kitchen area, drinking vodka from the bottle, late one night when he'd got up to go to the toilet. She pretended it was water, but he could smell the alcohol on her breath. He suspected she was trying to get rid of the baby. He wondered again whether Emily Baxter might have been trying to get rid of her baby.

He rebuked himself for his attempt at trying to assuage his guilt, to make what he'd done somehow less evil. The truth was, he knew, that he had murdered Emily and her baby and no reasoning could ever make it less than that. Even if the baby had been out of the picture, he had still killed... Whether it was one person or two was neither here nor there... he was a murderer. *Murderer... murderer... murderer...*

Chapter 20

Nigel didn't see Kelly again for six months. By that time, his divorce was finalised and his daughter had phoned him to say that they were going to sell the house and buy somewhere smaller for June. He felt relieved that at last he might be seeing a bit of the money he'd put in to purchase it, and maybe even be able to buy a place of his own with the proceeds. But his daughter explained, 'We've talked to the solicitor and he thinks that Mum would be entitled to keep the whole of the net sale proceeds. She stopped working, to bring me and Toby up, and then she had to look after you when you were unwell. Now you're working, so you can support yourself. Mum won't be able to find a job at her age, especially since she has been out of the job market for so long. It's easier if you agree—'

'Hang on a minute,' he began, but then a flicker of anger began to rise in his veins and he flinched, remembering the power of that emotion and the damage it could do.

'There's no point arguing about it, Dad. If you've got money to throw at a solicitor to argue, then by all means do that, but we're not budging. Mum deserves the lot after what you put her through. Mum's solicitor is going to write to you about it. There's a Consent Order that you need to sign. Make sure you don't delay in sending it back; Mum's really stressed out about all of this. The sooner we sell the house and buy her another one closer to me and Eric, the better. We want her to have somewhere she can call her own, away from the past and all the memories. Then she'll feel better.'

'Wait.' He was incredulous, but he held back, restraining his temper. 'I have rights. Surely, I can get a share of the proceeds. I should get fifty percent.'

'Dad, what you have to understand is, there's a recession at the moment, and the house isn't worth as much as it would be in a more buoyant market. Mum has to move out soon, though, or her health is at risk. She's been depressed since the divorce. She doesn't like living in that big house all alone. She needs to be able to support herself. Count yourself lucky that you've got a job and a roof over your head.'

Nigel looked around the scantily furnished apartment with the yellowing wallpaper peeling from the walls and the cracked glass in the windows. 'Annabelle, I was the one who paid for that house. This is unfair.' His voice was quiet, subdued.

'Sorry, Dad. If you have any remorse for what you did to your family, you'll understand. You're the reason Mum left. You brought this on yourself.' With that, she put down the phone. Her words rang inside his head: ...*brought this on yourself... if you have any remorse...* They merged with more familiar words that lived with him: *Murderer... murderer... murderer...*

Nigel held on to the phone for a bit longer than necessary before sitting it in its holder. It was as if by putting it down, he was admitting that this was the day he finally lost everything. The way Annabelle had spoken to him had been cold, like a stranger. Perhaps they *were* strangers. The culmination of one night of blind rage; this is what it all boiled down to.

His mind worked it over to the back beat of *Murderer... murderer... murderer.* He had to find a solicitor to argue his case, to try to get some of the proceeds from the house sale. He was struggling to pay the rent and bills and to afford to eat. *I can't go on living this way.*

As he sat on the park bench one lunchtime, pondering his life and the misery that lay ahead, Kelly appeared and sat next to him.

'Hi, Nigel. How are you?'

'Kelly? I haven't seen you around for months... How are you?'

'I'm fine,' she said, her well-rehearsed smile fixed on her face —dazzling, almost inscrutable—but her eyes told a different story.

He couldn't help noticing her stomach. It looked the same size as when he'd last seen her. Maybe she'd recently had the child and was yet to shift the weight. He calculated in his head the time since he'd last seen her, and it worked out that she would have recently given birth. He didn't want to mention anything, as she did not have the baby with her. Had she gone ahead with the abortion in the end? He decided to remain silent and let her lead the conversation.

After a few moments, she said, 'I've split up with Marty. He's thrown me out. It didn't last very long when he found out I was pregnant. He thought I was just a little overweight when we met. I've been staying with a friend for a couple of weeks, but she needs me out.'

'Oh. You could try the local council,' he said quickly, fearing she would ask if she could move back in with him again.

'Three months pregnant and out on the streets,' she said as if she hadn't heard him. He could smell alcohol on her breath and noticed that she was swaying slightly, a distant look in her eyes as she moved closer to him on the bench.

Then he realised what she'd said: "Three months pregnant." *How?* His thoughts felt muddled.

'Kelly, when are you due to have the baby?'

'Look, I don't want to talk about it, okay!' she snapped—it was very out of character for her to show anger. He'd never seen her lose her temper before. Her brow creased and she glared at him.

She's drunk, he thought. Then it occurred to him that she may have lost the baby because she had been drinking so heavily. He remembered catching her with the vodka bottle in his flat. Maybe she was pregnant again, after losing the other one? Maybe this was her new boyfriend's child? Maybe the easy answer was that she had kept the weight, not lost the bulge after the miscarriage. That would explain her anger. He thought it best not to pry.

'How have you been?' she asked, disinterestedly, folding her arms and leaning back on the bench, one leg crossed over the other.

'I'm bearing up,' he said, taking a bite of his sandwich. As he munched, he continued, 'My divorce came through.'

She twisted on the bench and looked him in the eye, her red hair unkempt and wild-looking. 'Oh? So you're a free agent? Want to go out with me?' She was smiling, and her eyes were as wild as her hair.

Nigel laughed.

She appeared offended, her eyes widening. 'What? What's so funny? I'm not good enough for you? Is that it?'

He stopped laughing and looked at her, surprised by what she'd said. Her eyes were full of unshed tears.

'Um... It's just that I'm twice your age. Old enough to be your dad. Don't you remember you once said I remind you of your grandfather? I mean, you don't want to be going out with your granddad now, do you?' He laughed again, but this time more nervously, afraid of what her reaction would be.

'What does age matter?' she said. 'We're all going to die in the end, and we don't know when. I could die tomorrow, and you could live until you're a hundred; age doesn't mean a thing.' She was waving her arms around as she spoke.

Nigel didn't know how to respond. He was concerned that maybe Kelly had taken some drugs. She didn't seem the same. Her stare was very intense yet very distant at the same time, and that edge of anger was threatening to erupt.

'So, what do you say, Nigel baby? Can I come and live with you again?'

'Um... I don't think that would be a good idea.'

'Why?' She got up off the bench and stood in front of him.

'I'm... I'm moving out soon,' he lied. 'I might be getting back with my wife. I have to go and see her and try to work things out properly.' Anything to stop Kelly staring at him like that.

'But you just said your divorce came through.'

'Yes.' He avoided her eyes as he spoke. 'It did. When the divorce came through, June and I both realised that we'd made a big mistake. We still love each other.'

'Well, that is actually very romantic. But if you're leaving, we have to give you a decent send-off. How about we get together and go out somewhere? Make a day of it. I wouldn't want you to leave London without spending some time with you. We're friends, Nigel. I'm going to miss you. Friends have to stay in touch.' She was swaying as she stood in front of him.

Nigel was unsure why she was saying these things. They hadn't seen each other for over six months, and even when she'd stayed with him, she was hardly there. They didn't spend any time together. Maybe she was just grateful that he'd let her stay at his flat, he thought. What harm could it do to spend a day with her?

'Can you drive, Nigel?'

'I haven't driven for years...'

Twenty, to be precise...

'I've just bought a car. Well, actually my last boyfriend gave it to me. I don't know how to drive. I didn't tell him that. Didn't want him to take it back. Looks expensive. He's quite rich. I wondered if you could take me for a drive in it. Maybe you could drive me out of town, to where you used to live? I'd like to see the sea. I haven't seen the coast for years. I used to live near the sea when I was growing up. Brighton. I loved all that; the ocean breeze, the seagulls, fresh fish. Maybe we could take a drive. You used to live near the sea, didn't you? Before you moved to London?'

'I haven't driven for years...' he repeated, knowing he would not feel comfortable getting into a car and driving.

'It'll be like riding a bike,' she laughed. 'Well, okay, it won't be, but you know what I mean. It's second nature, once you learn how to drive, you never forget...'

'I'm not sure,' he said, but his voice seemed to go unheard.

Kelly was still swaying in front of him, dreamy-eyed as if thinking of her adventure by the sea. She said, 'How about this weekend?'

'I'm not sure,' he repeated.

'Oh, come on, it'll be fun.' She pulled at his arms. 'We'll go and eat at a seaside restaurant. Fresh fish! We'll listen to the sound of the sea and take in the fresh salty air. All this pollution in London is no good for me, or the child growing inside of me...' She touched her stomach, and again Nigel wondered how she could still only be three months pregnant. She took his hands in hers and looked into his eyes. Her eyes reminded him so much of the biggest mistake he'd ever made. Somehow, he knew he would have to do this one thing for her. Everything about Kelly made him remember Emily. And, strangely, he felt that he was in some way making amends for what had happened—what he had done to Emily—whenever he helped Kelly. Although, if he was being honest, he knew that nothing in this world would ever put right what had gone wrong there. Nothing.

Chapter 21

At just after 4 p.m. that afternoon, Nigel was seated at his desk in the office, his back to the door.

'Nigel?'

Kelly? he thought, feeling quite startled. He turned around to see her standing at the door. His eyes widened. 'Kelly? I thought you didn't work here anymore.'

'Er... you must have me mixed up with someone else. I'm Emily. Don't worry, I do it all the time. It's such a big place, I'm always forgetting names and calling people by the wrong name,' she giggled, but appeared slightly nervous, her cheeks reddening. 'Are you Nigel?' she asked.

A paranoid fear gripped him and he stood up, backing away from her slightly. *Did she really say her name is Emily?* He couldn't be sure. So much of his mind was full of memories of that night. The name Emily barely left his consciousness... it was always floating there along with the other voices: *Murderer... murderer... murderer...*

She stood waiting for a reply.

As he caught his breath, he said, 'Um... yes, I'm Nigel. But we've definitely met before and your name's Kelly, right?' He was speaking his thoughts, fear taking control of his voice.

She frowned, her eyes darting from side to side as if she were unsure where to rest them. 'I'm Emily, I work in forensics. Perhaps Kelly looks a bit like me? As I said before, it's easy to mistake someone for another person in this place.' She spoke quickly, avoiding his eyes. 'I was told that you're the person who can photocopy some papers for me. I need them rather urgently.' She held out a file towards him, now daring to look him in the eye.

He reached out and took the file from her, sure that he was imagining this. He started to doubt himself. *Perhaps I'll wake up in a moment and find I dozed off in my chair. I really must try to go to bed earlier...*

He could hear his heart thumping in his ears as he took the file of papers from the girl.

'Can you have these ready in about an hour, please? I'll pop back and get them.' She smiled and left the room quickly as if eager to escape from his vacant stare.

Nigel was left bewildered. *My mind's playing tricks on me, that's all.* He took a deep breath, sighed, and walked over to the photocopier with the file of papers, his thoughts still whirring. He placed the blue lever arch file on the bench that sat in the middle of the room, and with trepidation he opened it. The first thing he saw was a newspaper article about Emily Baxter's case. It was yellowed with age. As he nervously flicked through the file, he noticed it was filled with every bit of news he'd ever heard about the case. He began to recall June's obsessive regurgitation of each feature that appeared in the newspapers. These stories dated back almost twenty years. It didn't make sense. Why? What was happening? Then he remembered he had seen news about the case being reopened. Perhaps his employers were involved somehow in the legal side of things.

He looked at the clock. It was 4.15. Emily... that girl, had said she would be back to collect the papers. But this was all too absurd. Surely it couldn't have happened. She was dead. Was she a ghost? More and more, he was starting to believe that she was haunting him. He kept seeing her. He'd murdered her, so her soul was not at rest... that must be it. She would follow him to the bitter end... drive him mad. She was taking revenge for what he had done. His rational mind began to argue against that. He didn't believe in ghosts. When people died, they died. Ashes to ashes. Still there was no explanation why an Emily Baxter look-alike had just walked into his office and handed him a file of papers relating to Emily Baxter's case. *What's going on?*

Just as he began placing the ragged sheets of newspaper onto the photocopier, Abigail entered the room to bring the day's post.

'Hi Nige, how's it going?' she said, swooping over to the sorting box and placing a bundle of envelopes in there. Then she stood, wrapping her golden ringlets around her fingers and smiling at him. 'It's been a busy day in litigation today,' she sighed, rolling her eyes.

He turned around to face her, not really in any mood to talk, his mind still full of eerie, unexplained thoughts.

'You look pale, Nige, are you okay?'

'Me? Er... yes, I'm fine,' he said, forcing out his best fake smile and dusting it off.

'This room is so stuffy with the photocopiers. You should ask them to get some air conditioning fitted. It can't be easy working in all this heat. I only pop in for a few minutes, and sometimes feel like I'm going to faint.'

'Oh, I'm used to it,' he said, shrugging.

'You don't look well.' She frowned. 'There's a nasty bug going around. Maybe you've caught it? Three people in my department were off sick today, hence the uber-busy day. I've had to do all their work! Ken's feeling a bit under the weather, too.'

Abigail and Ken were now an item, and she would often spend time chatting to Nigel about him. Since his breakup with June and the divorce, he wasn't really in the mood to talk about love and romance, but Abigail seemed to want to tell the world about her new man and she was constantly thanking Nigel for "convincing" her to go out with Ken. *'I had my doubts about him, but I'm glad I listened to you and gave him a chance. He's a great bloke and we're made for each other!'* she would say.

Abigail continued speaking: 'We're supposed to be going on a romantic break to Venice next weekend. I'm hoping he hasn't caught this bug... and that I don't get it!' She crossed the fingers on both her hands and held them up for Nigel to see. 'So, are you busy today?'

'Um... well, I just have a bit of photocopying to do,' he glared at the A4 file that was taunting him on the desk. 'For the forensics department,' he added, glumly.

Abigail frowned. 'I remember you saying that you thought we have a forensics department a few months ago. I asked Ken about that one day and he said that there isn't one.'

'Um... I thought she said *forensics*.' Nigel could still picture the girl standing there as real as Abigail was now. He felt his muscles tense.

'Oh well, I'll let you get on,' said Abigail cheerily, walking towards the door. 'I have mounds of work to catch up on, and I also promised Ken I'd take him up a cup of coffee. See you soon.' With that, she exited the room and left Nigel feeling perplexed.

He needed to find out for sure if there was a forensics department.

He took his mobile out of his pocket and dialled Bainsworthy's number.

'Good afternoon, Bainsworthy and Co. Solicitors; how can I help you?'

'Hello, can I speak to someone in the forensics department, please?'

'Um...' The receptionist paused. 'Sorry, sir, this is Bainsworthy Solicitors; are you sure you have the right number?'

'Yes.' Nigel's eyes widened. He felt a need to prove to himself that he hadn't imagined Emily's visit today. 'Forensics, please,' he said, a hint of desperation in his voice.

'One moment, sir, I will put you through to our criminal department; they might be able to help you. We don't have a forensics department as such.'

The line went silent as he was placed on hold.

'Bainsworthy, Criminal Litigation, can I help you?' came a voice that sounded as if it belonged to an elderly woman.

'Um... I hope so. I'd like to speak to someone in the forensics department, please.'

'I think you've been put through to the wrong department.' Then he heard her ask a colleague: 'Jen, there's a man on the phone asking to speak to someone in the forensics department. What's the extension?'

'Forensics? We don't have a forensics department. We're not the police! He must have called the wrong number.'

The elderly woman returned to the phone. 'Sorry, sir. I've checked with my head of department and we don't have a forensics department. Do you have a name of somebody you need to speak to?'

'Um... Emily.' He felt himself tremble as he said her name.

'No, there's no Emily here. Sorry, sir.'

As Nigel put down the phone, his brain was trying to make sense of everything. On the one hand, he was glad that there was no forensics department and no Emily, it had all been a dream— or he'd had a hallucinatory episode brought on by his stress and guilt. He remembered how the doctor he'd seen at the hospital after his nervous breakdown had explained to him that the brain could do amazing things, and sometimes what we see is not real, and when people are going through nervous breakdowns it's not uncommon for them to imagine seeing things that are not there. Although it eased his mind, to some extent, having an answer to the problem, it did not make the problem go away. He was painfully aware that the only other time he'd had such hallucinatory experiences was when he had a nervous breakdown, and he did not want to go through that again.

He could not shake the image of Emily standing there in his office. He tried to rationalise it: the guilt he felt over her murder was something that had not yet been dealt with and he had not admitted his part in her death to anyone, so his mind was stuck there remembering what he'd done. His grief and guilt were so great that images of Emily were manifested, and perhaps his mind was somehow using that as a way of helping him to come to terms with everything. But he knew that this was something he would never be able to come to terms with. So, what would happen now? Was he headed for another nervous breakdown like the last time? Maybe it was time for him to own up. Maybe he should go to the police now that they had reopened the case. He would be saving them time and resources; he'd be doing the right thing. He stood up and began to pace his office, nervously. He didn't want to be locked up in prison, with his mind torturing him daily for what he had done. He was already paying a high price for the murder. He'd lost his family, everything he cared about. June. His children. His home. He didn't want to lose his liberty as well.

His thoughts became disturbed as he began to ponder again whether it was in fact Emily's spirit that was haunting him. But he quickly pushed that thought aside, not allowing himself to explore that line of thinking. *Ghosts don't exist. There is always a rational explanation for everything.*

He sat down on his chair and took deep breaths—a relaxation technique he had tried in the past that had sometimes worked. As he began to feel calmer, a black thought gripped him: *Kelly had also said she worked in the forensics department... so if it doesn't exist, neither does she...* It had been a one-off meeting with Emily, but he had seen Kelly numerous times over the past year, and had even lived with her for a couple of weeks. How could *that* have been imagined? He felt cold, and goose pimples began to erupt on his skin. This realisation was too much for his mind to formulate. *Kelly is real... she has to be real...* Then he remembered that he had agreed to meet her this weekend.

He stood up and walked towards the table where "Emily" had left the A4 folder. It wasn't there. He searched his desk and everywhere else he could think of in that tiny room. It had disappeared. *What's going on?* A shiver raced through his body and beads of sweat formed on his brow.

Chapter 22

Kelly didn't arrive at the weekend. Nigel sat at his window, staring out at the street below, his mind in chaos. He wanted to pack his bags and leave, but where would he go? If he had just imagined this girl, Emily, he would not be able to run. She would always be there, haunting him.

In his more rational moments, he knew that he should seek help. He needed therapy, but that would mean handing himself in to the police and facing his demons head on. His greatest fear—the one that had stopped him confessing everything all those years ago—was that he would end up alone, in a cell, with nothing but the walls to look at; he would be living with his tortured soul and mind. Ironically, what he had been running away from had found him; here he was, living alone in a small studio flat, working alone in a small office, staring at walls, living with the guilt and remorse in his mind.

What if it was true that Emily had come back to haunt him? Would she ever leave him alone and give him any peace? Maybe her spirit had come back with the intention of taking revenge. Fear gripped him, and he looked behind and around himself in the small room as if expecting her to be there. Ever since seeing her in his office he had been paranoid, expecting her to turn up wherever he went.

He turned back to face the window and stared out, thinking these muddled thoughts. He was hoping that Kelly would not show up. He wanted to break the cycle. Even if it was true that he'd imagined his meetings with her, or if she had been some sort of phantom, he felt that now he had woken up and realised something wasn't right, somehow it would mark an ending to all of it. Maybe she could hold no further power over him now that he had figured out she wasn't real. He wanted to begin again and leave that chapter behind him. He didn't want to see her again, even if she was real; her face was too similar to Emily's and had brought back all the memories. Maybe that had been the problem from the start. Maybe when he'd first seen Kelly, because she looked so much like Emily, some part of his brain had latched onto that and begun to play tricks on his mind.

As much as he felt relieved that Kelly hadn't arrived, his thoughts began to drift to the negative aspect of her non appearance. Okay, so Kelly looked like Emily and, ideally, he'd prefer not to be reminded of her, but when all was said and done, Kelly—if she was real—was his only real friend. The fact that she hadn't turned up when she said she would didn't say much about their friendship. She hadn't even phoned to say why she couldn't come. He knew she had his mobile number, even though she'd never given him hers. He'd given his number to her when she asked if she could move in with him. Maybe she'd lost it.

The more he thought over everything, the more he began to feel foolish for ever doubting Kelly was a real person. He had been so caught up with the memory of Emily, just because Kelly looked like her, that he had inflated it out of all proportion so that Kelly seemed to represent Emily. Every time he saw her, his memories and the guilt would take over. He began to pace the living area of the small flat, praying that Kelly would show up. He wanted to prove to himself that he had made a real friend, that there was at least one person in the world who needed him despite his best efforts to keep himself segregated in his own private hell.

If Kelly comes, I promise I will stop associating her with Emily. He did not know who he was making this promise to. He had accepted years ago that there was no way God would ever listen to him again, not after what he had done. Perhaps if he could start looking at Kelly without automatically thinking of Emily, they would have a better relationship? Had that been what had freaked Kelly out? Maybe he'd said something or looked at her in a way that had turned her off him at their last meeting. So many times when he'd looked at her, he'd felt he was looking at Emily; what if he'd inadvertently offended her? He sat back down on the chair next to the window and saw the world outside that seemed so alien to him. He hardly ever really *looked* at anything anymore. He just kept his head down most of the time, and it was all he could do to keep control of the voices in his head. He didn't have enough concentration left to really see what was going on around him. Kelly changed that. When she was around, it was like he almost clicked back into the real world. He was forced to interact with another human being. She was like a lifeline to the real world, the world outside his mind. She was the only person that he ever really spoke to, the only one who'd said she trusted him. *Maybe I can persuade her to change her hair colour, and maybe even cut her hair. Then she wouldn't remind me so much of Emily.*

Nigel continued to wait in vain for Kelly to arrive, impatient now to see her again and to start their friendship anew. They had got off on the wrong foot, and it was all his fault. He would make it up to her. But then Nigel remembered her suggestion at their last meeting that she move in with him again, and part of his perfect tapestry for a new life was torn away; he realised he could not risk getting too close to her. He didn't want to give her the wrong idea.

His mind began to go off on another tangent. What would be so wrong about having a relationship with Kelly? Okay, she was young, much younger than him. She was probably about the same age as he had been when he had killed Emily. He had stopped living then. He didn't feel worthy of a life. He was too cowardly to kill himself, even though he had considered it many times. For the most part, he felt that his life had ended on the night he killed Emily. Would it be fair for him to start a new relationship now? To experience the joy of love? He shook his head. He knew he could never allow himself that luxury. He could not offer Kelly anything but an arm's length relationship. He had become too cold for anything more profound.

He felt himself blush, an odd feeling that he had not felt since he was a young man. Thoughts of Kelly and a potential relationship between them had stirred feelings that he thought were long since buried with the rest of his sanity. He had felt a stirring in his loins. How was it that the young woman who reminded him of the worst night of his life could also make him feel ecstatic thoughts?

He stood up and went over to the kitchen area to drink a glass of water, becoming hotter at the thought that Kelly could knock on his door at any moment, and here he was unable to switch off these feelings of lust. He drank the water, and began to think that maybe it was best that she hadn't turned up, after all.

When he sat by the window again, a sadness enveloped him as he contemplated cutting Kelly out of his life. He didn't want to completely lose her. He felt so alone. Up until the fateful night over two decades ago, he'd been quite a popular man. He remembered being described as "the life and soul of the party" once, and even though it was a comment from someone who didn't really know him, he'd been proud of the impression he had left on that person at the time.

After his troubled teenage years, he'd married June and settled in to life as a married man. He had gone out of his way to do exactly the opposite to what his parents had done, wanting to make sure that his house was full of life, and in no way reminiscent of the cold and uninviting place his former family home had been. He'd seen the start of his married life as a way to break free from all the chains that had bound him. He lost some of the anger that had been the hallmark of his personality as a boy. June only saw an outgoing, friendly, extroverted character when she met him, such was his desire to rid himself of the memories of the house he grew up in. He left home as soon as he could, first renting with Mike when they were at university, and then moving in with June quite soon after they met.

Most of the arguments he had with June in the early days of their marriage revolved around how he was too much of a socialiser. 'We're never alone,' she would complain, on a regular basis. But that was just it, Nigel didn't want them to be alone. Being alone brought back all the memories of the times he spent in isolation in his bedroom. He was determined to live. The way he saw it, his parents had not lived, they had only existed. They had put so many restrictions on themselves and on him because of their controlling behaviour. He felt like a wild animal who had been let out of a cage when he left home. At last he was free to be himself.

When he met June, it didn't take him long to decide that he wanted to get married. It was a way of proving to himself that he could be a better adult than his parents. He would do everything they should have done. He had it all planned in his head: he and June would have a big family and they would always have parties for the children and invite all their friends, buy them lots of toys. It was his way of rebelling, but he didn't realise that it was a destructive way to carry on. All the demands on his time caused by the endless socialising, and the long work hours, led to the stress that maybe could have triggered his act of rage—the act that put an end to any *life* he could have had.

When he had started hiding himself away from the world, his friends had drifted slowly away. He couldn't think of even one person he could call on now. Even Mike, his once best friend.

Memories of Mike flooded his consciousness, like an old wound that had been scratched and began to bleed.

They met on their very first day at primary school at the age of four. Nigel recalled how he'd had a red balloon, which Mike wanted. They'd ended up fighting over it and it burst. Nigel started crying, and Mike felt sorry for him. The next day, Mike brought two red balloons to school and gave one to Nigel. Their friendship was sealed. They did everything together. Memories of rock concerts they'd attended together sparked a nostalgic feeling. He recalled how Mike had almost been his guardian angel when he'd got into fights; Mike would always step in to save him. They both studied I.T. at university and even worked at the same company for two years after they graduated. Mike had married soon after that, and his wife had been relocated to York with her job, so he had moved up there to be with her. Nigel and Mike had stayed in regular contact and would often go on holidays together with their wives.

After the murder, Nigel had stopped phoning Mike. He had stopped returning his calls. A lifelong friendship was terminated, just like that. Mike had come to visit him about six months later and asked whether he had done anything to offend him. He appeared upset. Nigel said that he felt they had grown apart and didn't think they should keep in touch anymore.

'You're like a different person,' Mike had said, puzzled, as he stood outside the door of the home Nigel had shared with June.

'Maybe that's because I *am* a different person,' said Nigel, unable to meet his friend's gaze. He had always been able to talk to Mike about anything, and Mike had a way of eventually getting his secrets out of him. He trusted Mike completely, knowing he would always be on his side—that had always been the case, from the moment they'd met, through awkward teenage years— through thick and thin. Mike knew about Nigel's temper, but Nigel could not allow himself to tell Mike about this. He had to keep this to himself. The only foolproof way of doing that would be to break his ties with Mike. So he told a lie. 'I don't like Ruby,' he said. 'I've never liked her, and I wish you'd never married her.' He knew how much Mike loved his beautiful and kind-hearted wife.

'What has she ever done to you?' Mike sneered.

'I really think you should go now, Mike.'

'Wait!' He pushed the door to prevent Nigel closing it. 'You can't just say something like that about my wife and expect me to accept it. Apologise.'

'No. Just go home, Mike.'

'You've never said anything like this about Ruby before,' Mike's eyes were wide in surprise. 'What's changed?'

'She wears the trousers in your relationship.'

'What?'

'She relocates up to York and you follow like a sheep. You were working in London.'

175

Mike shook his head, baffled. 'Where has all this come from? You never said anything at the time.'

'Well, you were so under the thumb, you wouldn't have listened.'

Nigel saw rage in Mike's eyes. He had seen that before when they were out together and Nigel had got them into yet another fight. By the time they were in their late teens, Mike was tall and muscular, and only the most drunk or stupid louts would ever pick on him.

Mike had never looked at Nigel like this before; it was usually the way he would look at an enemy. Nigel began to worry that he would now use his anger against him. He could see a nerve in Mike's forehead twitching, just as it always did before he lost his temper. For a moment, Nigel loosened his grip on the door and felt himself drift forward towards his once best friend, *Perhaps if he hits me, if I can make him angry enough to punch me really hard, he would kill me and set me free...*

Mike stood at the door, his fists clenched, staring into Nigel's eyes with a searing look.

'You know, I'm glad you and Ruby moved away, I was just looking for a way to get you out of my life... You've been following me around like a puppy dog since we were kids,' snarled Nigel, hoping to enrage his friend. He closed his eyes, waiting for the punch.

'Huh! I've always been the one who has been there for you, Nige. Face it, without me you'd have no friends; you're a loud obnoxious jerk who usually says the wrong thing, and I've always had to get you out of tight corners. How many fights have I got you out of?'

'Don't flatter yourself,' Nigel retorted, anxious that the heat of the moment may have died down. Mike's fists were no longer clenched, his face seemed calmer.

Eventually, Mike shook his head and said, 'You know what? I'm not bothered. Stay away from me and Ruby. I feel sorry for June. You're an idiot.' With that, he turned on his heels and left.

Nigel never saw him again.

As Nigel reminisced about his old friend, the words floated back into his mind: *"without me you'd have no friends."* Mike had been right. He had no friends now. But he preferred that. There was just too much going on in his head. He couldn't talk to people, anyway. His paranoia never left his side. Whenever he spoke, he risked confessing all. It was all there on the tip of his tongue, always. A constant battle.

He found himself feeling depressed now that his one potential friend, Kelly, had deserted him. Then he began to worry. At their last meeting, she had been different. She had lost the baby; at least that was what he had concluded. She talked like a desperate woman. He remembered again how she had suggested that they should start a relationship. He frowned.

He reasoned that for a young attractive woman to be throwing herself at a has-been like him, she must have felt that she had no other option. What if she'd done something stupid? What if she'd killed herself? His eyes widened at the thought. It was a possibility. Especially if she had no friends and thought that he would be leaving London.

What had she been up to in the six months before their last meeting? *If she was out of work, had just lost her baby, felt all alone, and her only friend was leaving town, she might have...* He tried to stop the thoughts that would give him no peace. Standing up, he felt a compulsion to try to find her, help her. Somebody would know where she was. He could find out a contact number for her if he could find someone she used to work with at Bainsworthy. Or, he could find her last known address from the computer database. He cursed the fact that it was the weekend. The office was closed. He would have to wait until Monday to look up her details.

He decided to go and eat his lunch at the park. Perhaps he'd misunderstood Kelly when they'd last met. Maybe she was going to meet him at the park, rather than his flat. She'd said 12 p.m. It was now 1 p.m. Maybe she'd still be there.

Nigel quickly made himself a sandwich, wrapped it in cling film, and rushed out of the front door, almost running all the way to the park. Soon he felt out of breath. It had been years since he had last run anywhere, and his knees and the soles of his feet felt strained from the exertion.

On arriving at the park, he found that a young couple had taken up residence at his usual bench, so he walked further along the pathway and sat on the next bench, satisfied that from there, he could still see Kelly if she came into the park. He felt deflated that she was not there, and realised that since it was over an hour past their scheduled meeting time, it was unlikely that she would now turn up. Maybe she had been there but had left, thinking he wasn't going to turn up. He felt sad. *Why didn't I ask for her mobile number?*

He took the cling film off his sandwich and began to eat, keeping one eye on the park, hoping to see her. Would she come?

He finished off his sandwich, his hopes of ever seeing Kelly again slowly fading. When he stood up to leave, a young boy whooshed past him on a skateboard, leaving a breeze in his wake. Nigel brushed the crumbs off his trousers and began walking in the direction the boy had gone, heading for the park exit. The boy spun around on his skateboard to face him.

'Hello, Granddad!' he said, smiling.

Nigel now recognised him as one of the boys who had laughed at him when he had been sitting with Kelly on the bench. It had been a few months ago, but he could never forget that face; the face that had made him feel humiliated and old.

Nigel kept his head down and continued to walk, hoping to get back to his flat without any trouble. He felt nervous of young boys and teenagers, as he was getting on in years. Their youth was something that almost frightened him. And he read so many stories about young lads who carried knives, guns even.

As he walked towards the gates, trying to avoid looking up at the boy, flashes of scenes from the recent riots that had taken place in London, Manchester, and Birmingham, taunted him. The violence of those days had brought back to him the way that rage can take over and change a person's behaviour. He'd watched the news about those who had been arrested; many had been of previous good character. In his mind, it only highlighted and inflamed the fact that he had once been of good character. A long time ago. He now feared confrontation of any kind, as he truly didn't think he could trust himself. More than that, he feared the youth standing before him right now, and those like him, who thought intimidation was a way to stand out from the crowd; who thought being brash and loud was cool. He'd once been like that. Now, he was lost and dearly wished he could go back in time and tell his younger self to keep a low profile, not try to be something or someone bigger or stronger, but just hide. Maybe then, he would have lived a peaceful life. He would give anything for even one day without the continuous murmurs in his head blaming him constantly for taking a wrong turn.

But this boy who stood before him, one foot on his skateboard, grinning from ear to ear, had yet to learn his lessons. He had not fallen into the deadly trap yet, but the clock was ticking for him, and perhaps one day he would derail in the same way that Nigel had. Until that time, he was dangerous, and Nigel felt concerned as to what he was planning to do. Would he mug him?

The boy had grown a couple of inches since the last time he'd seen him.

'Are you on your own today, Granddad?' The boy laughed as Nigel shuffled past him. 'Say hello to your friend for me,' said the boy as he skated away.

Nigel shook his head, realising that the boy was harmless and he shouldn't have been scared. He'd just been having a dig about Kelly.

Nigel walked along the street, his head bowed. He saw the young boy stop up ahead and start to chat with another boy. They were standing at the corner of the street. Nigel had to walk past them in order to get to the road where he lived.

As he sidled past them, trying to act as inconspicuous as possible, not wanting to draw any attention to himself, he heard:

'Is that the old man who used to sit on the park bench?'

The young boy on the skateboard replied, 'Yeah, that's Granddad! He's not very chatty today, though.'

The boys' laughter rang in Nigel's ears. Turning the corner, he felt his cheeks redden.

That evening, Nigel's son, Toby, telephoned. 'Hi Dad, is it okay if I come and stay with you for a while? It's just for the summer months while I'm off uni.'

Nigel had not seen his son for almost a year. Since leaving home for university, he had disappeared from his life, apart from the odd phone call every couple of months asking for money. Other than that, he'd had no contact with him.

'Um... what about your mum?' Nigel closed his eyes, knowing that he was pushing his son away again, like he had done all his life, feeling unworthy of him.

'Mum's sold the house and is looking for another one. She's moved in with her new man, and I don't really want to get in their way.'

Nigel's mind became blank. *New man?* He had no idea that June was even seeing someone. Now, she had moved in with someone. They had only divorced a month ago.

'Er... your mother is living with someone?'

'Yeah, his name's Vincent. They met at Annabelle's wedding. He's a friend of Eric's dad. Seems like a nice man. Which is more than I can say for Eric. What does Annabelle see in him?'

Annabelle, Nigel's daughter, had married a couple of months ago; Nigel wasn't invited to the wedding. Annabelle had phoned him to explain why: *'Dad, I do feel quite bad about not inviting you, but I'm only thinking of Mum. I can't have both of you at the wedding. She's really taking the divorce badly. I don't want to upset her.'*

Nigel had not really felt anything but indifference after that conversation. He had never allowed himself to get close to his children, and consequently wasn't too concerned about missing Annabelle's wedding. So when Toby called asking if he could stay with him, Nigel was more than a bit surprised. He didn't really want Toby staying with him. He couldn't start being a father now after all this time.

'Toby, I only have a studio flat. If you stay here, you'll have to sleep on the floor.'

'Hmm... well, I don't have much choice. I haven't got anywhere else to stay as of next Monday.'

"Can't you look for somewhere to rent?" is what Nigel wanted to say, but he didn't. Another consequence of feeling unworthy of his children was that he always did what they asked, regardless of how it would affect him.

'I suppose you could stay for a while, see how it goes.'

'You're a life-saver, Dad. I'll drive up at the weekend and bring my stuff. Then, me and some friends are going on holiday, to Ibiza, for a couple of weeks. I'll be back after that.'

When Nigel put down the phone, some part of him actually believed that Toby was coming to stay with him at the best possible time—a time when he needed company to stop him tipping completely off the edge. If he'd been a religious man, he would have called it divine intervention: God answering his prayers and sending him someone to stop him feeling so alone and isolated. But he was not a religious man. Not since the 19th of August 1991, anyway. Before then, he had believed in God and he had done his best to avoid His wrath. After his fit of rage and the ensuing murder, Nigel had stopped believing. It didn't bear thinking about. After all, if God existed, he would certainly be going to Hell for what he had done and would burn in eternal fires and damnation. He preferred to believe that when someone died, that was it. It was easier to think that way. Beyond that, he refused to contemplate. It was like a dark curtain that remained drawn, lest opening it would reveal that there was nothing but doom and terror beyond it.

Chapter 23

Toby arrived late in the afternoon the following Saturday, in an old car that looked as if it had been rescued from a scrap yard. One of the doors was blue, but the rest of the car was green and the patchy paint work on the bonnet and back bumpers indicated it had seen a few scrapes in its time.

The car was full to the brim with plastic bags packed with clothes and shoes, CDs, books, and other personal belongings.

Toby asked Nigel to help unload the car. He was surprised that Toby had made it to the flat in one piece; it was unlikely he'd had any view at all out of the back windscreen as his belongings were packed in so tightly.

After half an hour of lugging untold items up to the third floor studio flat, Toby and Nigel took a break. They sat together on the old sofa bed in front of the portable TV.

'Wow! Is that a black 'n' white TV? I thought they'd stopped making those in the seventies!' said Toby, laughing.

'It's not black and white; the aerial just needs adjusting,' said Nigel, twiddling one of the knobs on the TV until some of the colour reappeared on the fuzzy screen.

'So, how have you been, Dad?' asked Toby, catching him off guard as he stood up to return to his seat on the sofa bed.

Nigel couldn't recall the last time any of his family had asked him how he was. He couldn't help wondering if Toby was just making small talk or trying to butter him up before another request for cash. After all, he was going on holiday with his mates this evening and would need some spending money.

'I'm okay,' said Nigel, somewhat grimly.

'I was sorry to hear about you and Mum splitting up, but it actually makes it easier for me to fit in at uni now,' he laughed as he spoke. 'None of my friends have parents who are still married.

Most of them don't even know at least one of their parents. I was feeling a bit like a freak.'

'Hmm... very funny,' said Nigel.

'Dad, I'm being serious.'

Nigel stood up. 'So, your mum has moved in with someone?' The idea of June living with another man had been constantly on his mind since he'd heard about it the week before. He couldn't help picturing her in another man's embrace. It caused him anxiety knowing that he had driven her into another man's arms. His mind was mixed up, in turmoil. There was no way to turn back the clock and be the husband she had wanted; it was understandable that she would look for love elsewhere. He couldn't help wondering whether she had been seeing someone all those years behind his back while they were still living together. Somehow, the knowledge that she had so easily entered into a relationship with another man after their divorce left his mind questioning whether she had been as chaste as he had imagined her to be during their marriage.

'I went to see them before coming here, actually,' said Toby. 'They don't live far from London. Essex. A small village. She seems happy. She told me to say hello to you. She wants you to know that there are no hard feelings.'

Nigel's eyelids dropped. Good old June, always thinking about how he was feeling. If he had been alone, he may have begun to cry, but not wanting his son to witness his tears, he turned around to face the kitchen area. 'Would you like a cup of tea? Coffee?'

'I wouldn't mind another cup of tea. I had some tea at Mum and Vincent's. Mum made a fantastic cheesecake.'

Nigel was glad to have a moment to himself as he stood at the kitchen bench, making the tea. Toby was still seated on the sofa bed, watching the TV. Thoughts whizzed around Nigel's head. He did not think that it would bother him if he found out that June was living with someone else, but when he had first heard about it, it was like an explosion in his brain. It was so hard to come to terms with. He knew that the main reason he was finding it so hard to accept was because he had been to blame for the marriage breakdown.

As he stirred the cup of tea he had made for his son, he suddenly wished he could be alone. He felt uncomfortable having his son in the room. He made up his mind to try to avoid conversation with Toby as much as possible, and he hoped that he would be leaving soon.

When Nigel returned to the living area, Toby had his feet up on the coffee table. He moved them when Nigel placed the tray, containing two cups of tea and a few biscuits, on the table.

'Did you know that Annabelle's pregnant?' said Toby.

Nigel's first thought, as always when he heard the word *pregnant* was of Emily Baxter; then he thought of Kelly. A darkness fell over him. Would this curse ever be lifted?

'Er... yes, I knew...' he lied, feeling embarrassed that his daughter hadn't relayed the news to him. He was always the last to know anything that happened in the family.

'That means she'll probably stay with Eric. I was hoping they would divorce,' said Toby. 'Although maybe they'll divorce anyway. These days, people still split up even if they have babies together. Happens all the time.'

'Toby. That's unkind,' said Nigel.

'Do you like Eric?' Toby raised his eyebrows as he chewed a soggy biscuit. A crumb fell out of his mouth and onto his jeans. He picked it off and ate it.

'I met him when Annabelle brought him home a couple of times last year. They seemed happy together.'

'He's a weirdo,' said Toby, taking a gulp of his tea.

'Your sister—'

'Is a weirdo, too... I know,' said Toby, giggling. 'They're perfectly suited.'

'I was going to say that your sister loves him. That's all that matters. You don't have to live with him.'

'Thank God!' blurted Toby. Then he looked at his watch and stood up. 'Dad, I'd better go. I'm meeting Joe, a friend of mine, at the airport in about an hour.'

'Okay. Um... have a good time,' said Nigel, standing up to face him.

'Yeah. It should be good.' Toby smiled. 'A group of us are going.'

'Don't get into any trouble out there,' said Nigel.

'We won't. I won't do anything you wouldn't do!' He winked at Nigel.

Nigel closed his eyes briefly.

'Oh, Dad, I'd better give you my car keys. I'm going to leave the car here. It's a bit temperamental; if I don't drive it every day, the battery goes flat. And you'll have to inflate the tyres once a week. Can I leave it with you to do that? Just drive it around the block a couple of times a day, that should be enough.'

Nigel took the car keys from Toby as if he were being handed a lethal weapon.

'I haven't driven in nearly twenty years,' he said, thinking out loud.

'Oh, it's like riding a bike,' said Toby as he made his way to the door. 'See you in two weeks, Dad.' He closed the door behind him, and Nigel's heart jumped.

The car keys glistened in his hand like the edge of a sharp sword. He walked over to the window of the flat and looked down at the car that he would have to drive. Fear shook him to the core.

***

A few minutes after Toby had left the house, there was a knock at the door of Nigel's flat. *Oh, he's probably forgotten something*, thought Nigel as he walked towards the door. He realised that he was becoming more comfortable with the thought of his son being around. Maybe things were changing for the better. Having Toby around, with his constant jovial chatter, meant less time for Nigel to be alone with his thoughts. He felt his mood lift for the first time in years.

He opened the door, but didn't see Toby. It was Kelly. She had turned up after all, even if it was a week late. Another positive thought. All of this felt alien to Nigel's brain, being so used to the dark thoughts that consumed him and wallowing in murky self-pity. He almost didn't recognise the new lighter emotions.

'Kelly... hello,' he said in a restrained manner, not wanting to fall into the mire of false hope. Were things really looking up for him, or was this just a temporary sense of false security?

'Nigel! Sorry I didn't come last weekend. I'm so glad you're still here! I was worried you'd have left London by now. I was feeling a bit sick last week. It must be the pregnancy.' She touched her belly, and Nigel noticed that it was quite large. He'd only seen her just over a week ago, and she'd only had a small bump. Perhaps it was the clothes she was wearing?

'I'm due any day now,' she said as she walked past him and into the flat. 'Sorry, I need to go to the loo—this pressure on my bladder is a pain in the... Sorry, I'll try not to swear!' She giggled as she disappeared into the bathroom.

Nigel closed the door and walked back into the living area. He was trying to calculate how long Kelly had been pregnant. It definitely made sense that she would be due any day now, as she seemed to have been pregnant for ever.

When she emerged from the bathroom, Kelly slumped onto the sofa and put her feet up on the coffee table, where Toby's had been not too long before. Thoughts of his son came to mind. What would Toby think if he returned to find Kelly in the flat?

'You wouldn't be an angel and make me a cup of tea would you, Nigel?'

'Um... of course,' he said.

Kelly's eyes surveyed the boxes and plastic bags scattered around the room: Toby's stuff. A frown wrinkled her brow. 'So, it's true? You weren't joking about moving back in with your wife, then?' Her voice had a moody tone.

Nigel had his back to her as he prepared the tea. He didn't know whether to continue with the lie, but then remembering how odd she had been behaving at their last meeting; he decided it would be for the best, otherwise, he might end up saddled with Kelly and her baby as permanent fixtures in the flat. As he thought about that, his mind began to taunt him: perhaps he was being selfish. Maybe the right thing to do would be to take Kelly in and look after her and the new baby as a way of making amends for what he had done to Emily. Maybe this was a chance for redemption. *But how could I look after them?* his mind screamed. *She looks so much like Emily, I would have to look at her every day and be reminded...* But then he tuned back into the chanting that never went away: *Murderer... murderer... murderer...* and he realised that whether Kelly was here or not, he would never forget.

'Yes,' he said slowly. 'I'm moving back home.'

There was silence for a couple of minutes. He walked back into the living area.

'Nigel, why do you have to leave?' said Kelly, standing up from the sofa, holding what looked like a hammer. *A hammer. The hammer.* It was the hammer he had hit Emily with; the one that had killed her. Blood was dripping from the edge, still red. *But how can that be?* He felt confused. The words in his head became louder: *Murderer... murderer... murderer.*

Kelly rushed towards him with the hammer and hit him on the head. He could see the blood dripping down the side of his face, into his eyes. There was a welcome relief from the warm liquid. At last, he had been freed! He felt his life slipping away from him. Things were hazy, becoming white... soon there would be nothing. *Bliss*, he thought. The voices had gone. He felt himself drifting away through nothingness that looked like clouds that had drifted down from a mountain somewhere.

'Nigel, why do you have to leave?' said Kelly. He blinked and saw that she was seated on the sofa bed with her feet up on the coffee table, just as she had been since he'd gone to make the tea. He stood holding the two cups of tea. No sign of the hammer or blood. He hated the way he seemed to lose control of his mind when Kelly was around. She triggered so many bad memories. He wanted her to leave.

'Nigel? Are you okay? You seem miles away.'

'Sorry,' he said, walking towards her and handing her a cup of tea.

He sat down on the armchair and stared at the fuzzy TV screen, his mind still full of the gruesome images that had been floating through it only moments before. Somehow, he felt a yearning to be free, to feel like that again. He had drifted off to a nicer place.

He shook his head back to the present day, aware that he risked going back into the catatonic states that were linked to his depression and breakdown years ago.

He noticed that the TV still looked black-and-white even though he had tried to adjust it. He avoided Kelly's gaze but could see from the corner of his eye that she was looking at him. 'Nigel, can I come with you? I won't be any bother. I... I... You'll hardly know I'm there. It's just, I've got no one, and... and I'm scared.'

He was drawn to look at her then. Her eyes were wide and frightened-looking.

'Wh.. Why are you scared?'

'I don't want to have the baby alone. I know nothing about babies.'

'I'm sure if you contacted your parents, they be delighted to have a grandchild... even if you had your differences in the past —'

'My parents are dead,' she interrupted.

'But...'

'I didn't tell you before, because I don't like remembering. They died in a car crash.'

189

Nigel's face paled, almost as if he felt guilty for killing Kelly's parents as well as Emily and her baby.

'I was only nine,' said Kelly, tears at the edges of her eyes.

'I'm so sorry to hear that... Who... Who brought you up?'

She was now staring at the fuzzy TV screen that had one black line repeatedly rolling up the screen. She appeared to be in a trance. 'My sister, Mandy, brought me up. She was sixteen when our parents died. But she had a nervous breakdown when she was twenty-five. Now, she's moved to Spain. She lives in the mountains and says the climate's better for her and that there's less stress over there. I used to visit her, but she finds it hard to see me because I remind her of everything. I haven't heard from her for five years. I'm too scared to try to contact her in case she's...'

Kelly stared at the TV as she had been doing for the past few minutes. 'In case she's...' She turned to look at Nigel. 'I used to have a recurring dream that I was at Mandy's funeral. She would be lying in an open casket, covered in roses that looked like blood. The dream started about a month after my parents' funeral, and I had it for years. She was all I had left in the world. I suppose I was afraid of losing her...' she paused. 'Anyway, now I'm too scared to try to get in touch with her, in case she's not there. The week before Christmas, five years ago, she phoned me to say that she had sent me a gift. We chatted, and she sounded better than ever. She'd just met a man, Pablo, and they were getting on really well. She said she would phone me on New Year's Day. She never did. I waited for her call. All day. Then I waited the next day, too. After a week, I was worried, but I tried to think of other things. I've been telling myself that she'll call; Mandy will call one day. Of course, I've moved since then, and she wouldn't have my number now, but you know, I still wait for her call. Sounds stupid, doesn't it?'

She was staring at him, waiting for a reply.

Nigel shook his head and lowered his eyes, the intensity of her gaze was almost frightening. 'Er... didn't you try phoning her at the time?'

'No, I couldn't. I was too frightened. I know I should have... I tried, but each time I picked up the phone I put it down again. I kept waiting for her call... She said she would call...'

'If you know where she lives, you could try getting a message to her. Maybe write her a letter,' suggested Nigel. 'She might be looking for you.'

Kelly continued as if she hadn't heard Nigel; she was staring at the TV screen again: 'I thought about flying over to Spain when I found out I was pregnant, but I couldn't do it to her. I can't ask that from her. She had to bring me and my little sister up when our parents died. I couldn't ask her to help bring up this child. Anyway, for all I know, she might have kids of her own by now, and if she is alive but hasn't contacted me in so long, maybe she doesn't want to keep in touch.'

'You have a little sister, too? Where is she?' asked Nigel.

'Sheri married young; she was sixteen. She has three children. She emigrated to Australia a few years ago, and I haven't heard from her since. I had a falling out with her husband: he tried to get me into bed when Sheri was pregnant with their second child. I never want to see him again.

'So, you see, I'm all alone in the world, Nigel. You're the only one who has ever been kind to me. You could save me.'

Looking into her brown eyes, he shook his head as memories poured into his consciousness. 'I can't help you, Kelly,' he said, almost as a way of blocking the memories, willing them to go away.

Her mouth fell open. Then she covered her face with her hands and took a deep breath. When she took her hands away from her face, he could see that tears were forming in her eyes.

'I trusted you, Nigel,' she shook her head. 'I've told you everything about me. I... I thought you could help, but you've let me down. I'm so disappointed.' Again, she covered her face with her hands, then wiped away the tears. She stood up and suddenly leaned forward, breathing quickly and loudly, gasping, 'Oh!... Oh... no!' she said between breaths. 'It's the contractions... they've started... oh... no! Nigel!' she screamed. 'Nigel! Help me! You'll have to take me to the hospital.'

'I can't!' he said. 'I don't have a car. I'll call an ambulance.'

'No ambulances!' she screamed and grabbed his arm. 'My parents both died in an ambulance... I can't. I need you to drive me. You have a car outside. I saw you earlier, taking things out...' She breathed deeply again.

'That's my son's car.'

'It's still there! Use it!' she pleaded.

'But I haven't driven in twenty years, and I don't have insurance...'

'Nigel! Get me to that hospital unless you want to deliver the baby here!' she screamed.

'I can't!' Nigel almost lost his temper, but stopped himself. It was beginning to get dark outside, and he could hear the pitter-patter of raindrops on the windows. Panic began to rise inside him. *I can't drive... 'but this is your chance to help Emily,'* came a voice he didn't recognise as his own. 'What?' he said out loud, trying to block the thoughts in his head.

Seemingly oblivious to his outburst, Kelly had now sat down on the sofa and was taking deep, measured breaths.

'Maybe it was a false alarm,' said Nigel, hoping with all his being that it was.

'No,' she shook her head. 'That was just the first one... I have to time them. She looked at her watch. 'It's definitely coming, Nigel.'

He sat on the chair next to the sofa bed.

'Don't sit down!' she screamed. 'You need to get a bag together for me. I need stuff. You'll have to phone the hospital and ask them what I need to bring. I've forgotten.'

Kelly began to scream as another contraction took hold.

'Look, it's too late now, we have to leave or the baby will be born in your flat!' She stood up slowly, leaning forward. 'Come on, Nigel.'

Half in shock, he stood up, trying to convince himself that this was just a dream.

I'll wake up soon, I'll wake up soon...

Walking down the flights of stairs to the front door felt like a walk to the gallows. He kept hoping Kelly would just have the baby there on the stairs. He wanted to call a neighbour, a passing stranger to help, fetch an ambulance... but she didn't want an ambulance...

The cold air hit him as they walked out of the old house and he realised that he was only wearing a T-shirt. He had been feeling hot earlier, helping Toby carry his belongings into the apartment, so had removed his cardigan.

He opened the door of the old car, eyeing it cautiously as if it were alive. Kelly sat in the passenger seat and he walked around the side of the car, his hand trembling as he tried to open the door. His fingers slid a couple of times as he tried to grip the handle.

Perspiration on his brow, he sat in the driver's seat, his body as stiff as a block of wood, as heavy as a ton of lead. He couldn't move. He was frozen to the spot, more from fear than the cold.

'Drive, Nigel! I can feel another contraction coming. Arrrgh!'

He heard her scream ring out. It echoed in his head, the sound becoming one with the memory of Emily Baxter's scream that night over twenty years before.

He fumbled to fit the key in the ignition and prayed the car wouldn't start. *'It's temperamental,'* Toby had said. It was his final hope that the car would not start, so they would have to use alternative transport.

Why didn't I just lie to her? Tell her I didn't have the keys? he thought as the engine began to roar. The stereo clicked into action, playing a moody rock song he had never heard before. He tried to turn off the stereo, but Kelly's hand reached the knob first.

'I love this song,' she said, turning up the volume and humming along between elongated breaths.

Nigel hadn't wanted music playing in the car, especially not loud rock music. Over the years he had often wondered if the same end would have occurred if he had been playing classical music, or something mellow, in the car, something that would have calmed him rather than fuelled his anger and rage. The one thing he couldn't do was go back and find out. It was just another way he found to torture himself over the killing.

Nigel reversed the car slightly to get out of the tight parking spot.

'The lights!' shouted Kelly. 'Turn the lights on!'

'Oh. S... s... sorry,' he stammered.

He could feel the adrenaline causing him to shake involuntarily as he eased the car out of the parking spot.

The local hospital was only a ten-minute drive, he reminded himself, trying to settle his nerves. As long as he stayed calm, he would be okay.

Nigel made his way towards the main road. The song faded out on the stereo and a familiar intro began... *How Will I Laugh Tomorrow*... began to play. As Nigel drove along the road, a strange thing happened: he found he was no longer on the main road in the London suburb, but instead, he found himself back on the old road, the deserted and dangerous road where he had killed Emily and her unborn child. *B... b....b... but how can this be?* He blinked a few times, but the scene remained the same. There was no other traffic, just him in the car with Kelly, on the dark deserted road.

'K... Kelly... I'm not sure... I'm not feeling very well,' he managed to say. 'I have to stop the car.'

'You can't! We need to go faster! Put your foot down!'

Nigel put his foot down on the accelerator and felt himself speeding along the dark road, potholes shaking the old car's suspension as he drove. Then, he heard a smash, loud sirens, beeping horns, but there were no other cars around. Where was it coming from? He looked around him. Then, all he saw was white light.

The local paper carried the story a week later:

Nigel Price, 56, died last Saturday evening when the car he was driving smashed head-on into a lorry. Mr Price was driving on the wrong side of the busy main road when the incident occurred. Witnesses say he was speeding. An eyewitness said he appeared to be talking to himself.

This would usually suggest that he was having a conversation on a hands-free mobile, but no mobile phone was found in the debris. Since the incident, two local schoolboys have come forward after recognising his face in the national news story. They say that they had often seen him talking to himself in the park.

Mr Price had recently been divorced from his wife and there is speculation that given his history of mental illness (he suffered a nervous breakdown and depression, some 15 years previously), he may have deliberately crashed the car. He was driving alone, so no one else is being investigated in this tragic accident.

He leaves behind two children.